-Book One-

MIDNIGHT REYNOLDS

AND THE SPECTRAL TRANSFORMER

-BOOK ONE-

MIDNIGHT REYNOLDS
AND THE SPECTRAL TRANSFORMER

CATHERINE HOLT

ALBERT WHITMAN AND COMPANY
CHICAGO, ILLINOIS

Library of Congress Cataloging-in-Publication
data is on file with the publisher.

Text copyright © 2017 by Catherine Holt
Cover illustration copyright © 2017 by Albert Whitman & Company
Cover illustration by Ayesha Lopez
Published in 2017 by Albert Whitman & Company
ISBN 978-0-8075-5125-7 (hardcover)
ISBN 978-0-8075-5126-4 (paperback)
Printed in the United States of America
10 9 8 7 6 5 4 3 2 1 LB 22 21 20 19 18 17

Design by Jordan Kost

For more information about Albert Whitman & Company,
visit our website at www.albertwhitman.com.

To Barry

Chapter One

To tail or not to tail, that was the question. Midnight Reynolds stood in front of the large oak tree where she always met her friends Sav and Lucy, and clutched at the long piece of fabric tied around her waist. It was the Friday night after Halloween—which had been Midnight's birthday, actually—and their school was having a dance, complete with costumes.

Definitely a tail, she finally decided. She tightened the fabric around her waist and smoothed down the furry mouse pants her mom had made, making sure her glasses were in the pocket. Thanks to a dry-eye condition that prevented her from wearing contact lenses, she needed glasses to see at a distance. Unfortunately, when the plain wire frames were combined with her straight, dark hair, sludge-green eyes, and snub nose, they made her look like a goblin. But Midnight carried them for extreme emergencies.

The school was dark, apart from the gym, which was glowing with lights. The doors hadn't opened up yet, and despite the cool night, several groups of boys were running around in short sleeves, screaming and yelling. The girls huddled together in clumps, pretending to ignore them. It reminded Midnight of a nature documentary.

As she waited, a familiar buzzing hummed in her ear. Midnight flinched. She'd first started hearing the noise just after they moved to Berry and had thought it was a power tool. The next time it had happened, she'd assumed it was her sister Taylor's phone ringing with a new (and really annoying) ringtone. But after the rest of her family didn't blink an eye, Midnight realized that whatever it was, no one else could hear it. Which was weird and creepy. She'd been ignoring it ever since.

There was still no sign of Sav and Lucy. She glanced at

the time on her phone. What if Sav hadn't forgiven her?

The whole argument had started over Logan Johnson, a boy that Midnight didn't even like. Well, not like that. But Sav did like him *like that*. She had been furious when Logan had called Midnight to ask for help with their science quiz.

The result was that Sav and Lucy had ignored Midnight for two days. Thankfully, just before second period, Lucy texted to say that Midnight could go to the dance with them and that they'd decided to dress up like mice. Hence the costume.

What if they'd sent her the text just to trick her?

Her stomach churned. It wouldn't be the first time she'd been humiliated. At her old school in Texas, Midnight had been teased mercilessly for her strange name and lack of money. Even thinking about the sneers and the teasing laughter caused a lump to form in her throat. But last year, her mom had inherited the house in Berry from her aunt Glenda, and they'd moved to West Virginia for a fresh start.

Fresh nightmare was more like it. Not only had her mom started dating Phil—a mechanic with a bizarre hobby of dressing up like a Viking, complete with chain mail and strange leather boots—but that was when the weird noises had started. The ones she refused to think about.

"Hey, what are you doing out here?" someone said, and Midnight jumped before turning to see Tabitha Wilson. As usual, Tabitha was all in black and wore her default smirk. They weren't exactly friends, but yesterday Miss Henderson had paired them up for a local history project.

Midnight frowned. "Waiting for friends. Anyway, why are you here? I didn't think a school dance would be your thing."

"Tell me about it. My mom's worried that I don't have enough school spirit. So it was either this or joining a sports team." Tabitha shuddered before pulling out her phone and bringing up a game. "But don't worry. I have no intention of dancing. I'm just going to sit by myself and level up on Zombie Cheerleaders. So, are we still on for tomorrow to start the project? I could come to your house if you like."

"Actually, could we go to yours instead?" Midnight

said out of habit. Her mom ran a vegetarian lifestyle vlog called *Vegelicious* and Saturday was filming day. That meant anyone who happened to wander into the kitchen found themselves somehow involved. "Or the library, we could just meet there."

"The public library on a Saturday?" Tabitha shuddered, sending her black hair out in all directions. "No thanks. Far too many kids and oldies. But you could always come to my place."

"That would be great."

"Cool. I'll text you the address and time," Tabitha said before walking toward the dance.

There was still no sign of her friends, and Midnight chewed her lip as she studied her phone. Should she text them, or would that make it worse?

She hit the screen, but before she could bring up Sav's number, a flash of bright white light flickered up from the side of the school like static electricity. She stiffened. It was coming from the side of the school that was dark and closed for the night. Midnight rubbed her eyes, but the building was about forty feet away and her lousy focus didn't improve. There were still a few huddles of parents talking among themselves, but no one else seemed to have noticed it.

There was another flash, this time accompanied by a buzzing sound more intense than she'd ever heard. It was as if a swarm of bees had been let loose right in her ear. Goose bumps traveled along her skin and she rubbed her arms, suddenly pleased to be wearing the extra layer of fake fur. Her efforts to ignore it didn't work, and the noise increased.

Another flicker of bright light shot up into the air, and still no one acknowledged it. What if it was a fire, and she was the only one who saw it start? Midnight took a deep breath and cautiously walked toward the building. The nearby trees groaned and creaked in the wind, which did nothing to calm her erratic heartbeat.

"Hello?" she called out as she neared the school. Her vision was still too blurry to make anything out, but she thought she saw someone moving in front of her. A thin wail pierced the air, followed by a scuttling noise, as if something went racing toward the administration wing. There was no sign of a fire, but the bright lights were still flickering along the side of the building like a faulty light bulb. The buzzing noise increased, and adrenaline flared through her body. Just as she was about to call out again, the buzzing came to a sudden stop.

Apart from the dull hum of music from the dance, there was silence. Whoever had been there was gone. She was just about to turn and leave when she spotted a gold locket and chain lying at her feet. Midnight picked up the necklace and looked around for its owner. The place was still deserted, so she slipped it into her pocket and made her way back past the building and over to the oak tree.

Sav and Lucy were waiting for her.

Midnight's stomach flipped. She'd come to Berry expecting to fly under the radar at best and be bullied at worst. She'd never had friends like them before— popular friends. But on her second day at school, she'd been seated with Sav and Lucy in science. Since they'd both been too busy playing on their phones to do the osmosis project, Midnight finished it on her own. She didn't mind. She'd seen popular girls in action before— it was better for her just to do the project and not have them mess it up. When her color-coded spreadsheet of results had ended up at the top of the class, Sav and Lucy stopped ignoring her. They laughed at her jokes and decided that they were going to adopt her. For the first time in her life, Midnight felt like someone other than her family could see her. The three of them had been inseparable ever since.

Until two days ago.

Her throat tightened, and she instantly forgot about the necklace and the strange light. As she got closer, she could see they were both dressed as mice. Unlike her own homemade costume, though, theirs were store bought, complete with matching rhinestone mouse ears. Lucy looked cute, but as always, it was hard not to notice Sav, with her pale blond hair and brilliant brown eyes, flecked with gold.

"H-hey." Midnight came to a halt and tried to ignore her shaking hands. "You're both here."

"Of course," Sav said. "Why? Did you think that we wouldn't show?"

Yes. No. Maybe.

"I hoped you'd come." Midnight took a deep breath and tried to sound confident. "And I just want to say once again how sorry I am."

"Stop." Sav held up her hand. "I'm the one who should be apologizing. I feel so dumb for letting a boy come between us."

"S-so you believe that I don't like Logan?" Midnight stammered as her breath caught in her chest. "Because I have a very long speech prepared to prove it to you, and—"

"You don't need the speech," Sav said. "I'm really sorry, Midnight. I should never have given you the silent treatment. I can't believe I thought I liked him. I'm totally over that. Please tell me that you forgive me?"

"Of course," Midnight said, relieved. "There's nothing to forgive. I'm just happy that we're all okay again."

Lucy grinned. "Actually, we're better than okay. Tell her about the skiing."

"Skiing?" Before this year, Midnight had spent her entire life in Texas, which meant she knew as much about skiing as she did about astral projection—nothing.

"My dad's rented a chalet in Rush Valley for the first week of January and I'm allowed to invite you and Lucy." Sav broke out one of her smiles that she reserved for her closest friends.

"Wow." The idea that she had just been invited to go skiing with Savannah Hanson, *the* most popular girl at school, was unbelievable. It was amazing. It was magical.

"So? Will you be able to come? Sav and I have already worked out a list of all the things we'll need to buy and it shouldn't cost more than two hundred dollars. Three hundred tops."

It was expensive.

Her stomach dropped.

Her family never had much money, and with her mom and Phil's upcoming wedding, they were on a budget. Midnight guessed that skiing wouldn't fall into the budget category.

"What's wrong?" Lucy's eyes narrowed. "Don't you want to go?"

"Of course I do. More than anything," Midnight said. Besides, it was only money. She'd figure out a way around it.

"That's great." Sav pulled out her phone. "We need to take a photo and then we can go and dance."

Sav's excitement was contagious and Midnight leaned

into the shot. She didn't care what she had to do to find the money. As the camera flashed, Midnight remembered the strange lights over by the school building, but she pushed it from her mind. Right now, all that mattered was Sav and Lucy were still her friends, and she grinned as the three of them headed into the dance.

CHAPTER TWO

As a rule, Midnight was a planner. Where Sav and Lucy blew their allowances on whatever caught their eyes, Midnight preferred to do the research, collect the coupons, and analyze it all on a color-coded spreadsheet. The fact that her allowance was only a quarter of the size of theirs had something to do with it, but she knew that a little bit of planning could go a long way.

Which was why she was sitting in the kitchen with her secondhand laptop, trying to systematically figure out a way to earn money.

"Wow." Her mom's fiancé Phil let out an impressed

whistle as he walked in holding the newspaper, a bag of her mom's favorite bagels, and what looked like a wooden Viking shield. "I didn't know you could even do things like that with a spreadsheet."

Midnight always knew that her mom was spontaneous. After all, she named her daughter Midnight just because she was born at twelve o'clock on Halloween. But now that spontaneity had also caused her mom to get engaged to some guy after just three months.

"She's an organizational wizard," her mom said, looking up from where she was coaxing a cake out of a round tin.

Midnight's sister, Taylor, who was three years older, dragged her gaze away from her phone. "More like a freak," she retorted from the other end of the stripped-wood kitchen table. The table and its mismatched chairs had belonged to Great Aunt Glenda, but the numerous pots and pans, recipe books, and green potted plants had all come with them from Texas. So had her mom's crystals, which were hanging in the window, flashing rainbows as they caught the weak morning sun.

"I can actually hear you." Midnight dipped the screen

of the laptop so that Phil couldn't see it. Taylor could call her a freak all she wanted, but it didn't change how great the previous night had been. The mouse costumes were a hit, the DJ had played their favorite songs, and Sav had told her more about the skiing trip. Which reminded her. She looked at the first idea on her list and gave her mom a hopeful smile. "What are your thoughts on increasing my allowance? For the ski trip?"

"Sorry, kiddo." Her mom pushed a strand of curly, blond hair behind her ear. "The next six months are all about the wedding and the honeymoon."

Midnight tried not to think about the honeymoon. She and Taylor were going on it too—a family-bonding trip to Charleston. Personally she'd rather visit the dentist than have to deal with all the speeches about how Phil wasn't trying to be a father replacement.

Her dad had died in a car accident when Midnight was one, so it wasn't like she even knew him. Her mom had been so sad that it was difficult for her to talk about him, which meant that all Midnight had were some photographs and grainy home videos.

But at least she had her mom.

Or at least, she used to. Everything was different now. No more having cereal for dinner or sneaking into her mom's bed during a thunderstorm or crying as they watched a sad movie. Instead, she had to make polite conversation with a guy who liked to dress up in chain mail and practice sword fighting in Berry Memorial Park every Saturday afternoon. Oh, and her mom—who'd previously shown no interest in Vikings whatsoever— had suddenly taken to wearing long dresses and watching YouTube videos on how to make flatbread.

Midnight sighed. "Okay, fine. I'll get a job." She'd already made up a flyer to do babysitting or yard work and a list of all the places she could put it. She wanted to get started today, but before she could do anything, she had to go to Tabitha Wilson's house to work on their project.

"Or, here's a crazy idea. You could actually say no to your friends," Taylor said. "You don't even like skiing."

"That's not true. Just because I haven't been skiing before doesn't mean that I won't like it. For all we know, I could be an amazing skier."

"I think you'll have a great time, Midnight." Phil handed her a bagel and then picked up his shield. It had a golden head painted on it. "I used to go each year with a group of Gunnars. Of course we used traditional pine skis and always ended with a battle."

The Sons of a Gunnar was the name of Phil's Viking group, and he talked about them. A lot. Midnight braced herself, but before he could say anything else, her mom, who'd finished with the cake and headed to the laundry room, walked back into the kitchen holding the mouse costume in one hand and Midnight's glasses in the other.

"Midnight Reynolds, for the hundredth time, could you please be more careful with your glasses? Or wear them? You know what the optometrist said. The longer you strain your eyes, the worse your sight will get." Her mom handed them back to her.

"I do wear them," Midnight protested, which wasn't exactly a lie. As long as no one she knew was around, she was happy to put them on. "Sorry. I'll be more careful in the future."

"Thank you." Her mom's brow furrowed as she pulled a gold necklace out of the costume pocket. "What's this?"

"Oh." Midnight had forgotten about the necklace, as well as the flickering white light and strange humming sound at the school. "I picked it up near one of the buildings and meant to hand it in at the dance. I guess I forgot."

Her mom held the locket up. As the morning sun streamed in, Midnight could now see it was engraved with small flowers. Her mom flicked it open to reveal an old black-and-white photograph of a woman with large, dark eyes and a warm smile on her face. The photo's background was black and smudged, like it had been darkened with age.

"Judging by all the lace around the neck of her blouse, this must be well over one hundred years old. The owner must be beside themselves with worry," Midnight's mom said.

"Hey." Phil joined them at the table and put his glasses on so he could study the photograph. "This person looks like Natasha Appleby—I bet it's one of her relatives."

"Who?" her mom asked.

"Sorry, sometimes I forget that you haven't always lived in Berry. Miss Appleby owns that big, two-story Victorian house on the corner of Garston and Hamlet.

I'll give her a call." Phil dug his phone from his pocket and walked into the next room.

Midnight turned her attention to her spreadsheet, but just as she was getting back to work, Phil walked back in, a grim expression on his face.

"The good news is that the locket does indeed belong to Miss Appleby," he said. "The bad news is that she broke her ankle on Friday, so she can't come to collect it."

"Is she okay?" Mom asked.

"She's at home, and she's recovering," Phil told them. "But she's so happy we found the necklace. Apparently it's the only photograph she has of her great-great-great-grandmother."

"Do you think she'd offer a reward?" Midnight asked.

Her mom shot her an annoyed look. "Midnight Reynolds, not everything's about money."

Taylor sniggered. "Yeah, Midnight."

"I'm sorry, she didn't say anything about a reward," Phil said. "Though she'd love to thank you in person for finding it."

Her mom turned to Midnight. "You could take the necklace back today."

"But I can't," Midnight protested. "I've got to go to Tabitha Wilson's house for our project."

"Miss Appleby only lives a few blocks from here. You can easily drop by." Her mom's lips were tight and her eyes were narrow. There was no way she was going to change her mind.

"Fine. I'll take the necklace to her before I go to Tabitha's." Midnight sighed while mentally adding one more thing to her to-do list.

Between school projects and running errands, would she ever have time to find a job?

CHAPTER THREE

A little while later, Midnight stood in front of Miss Appleby's two-story brick house, wishing she didn't have to be there. The only thing stopping her was that her mom would freak if she didn't return the necklace.

She sighed and looked up at the house. It had a neat, cobblestone path leading up to a wide porch and a cheery yellow front door. Around the side was a large rainwater tank, clearly visible above the white fence.

Her heart pounded as she walked up the path. If Sav and Lucy were with her, they would laugh at Midnight's nerves, but the truth was that she found it difficult to meet new people. It was part of the reason why she'd always struggled to make friends in the past. Well, that and the fact that she had a name like Midnight.

She lifted the heavy, black knocker and gave it three sharp raps. There was no answer, and she was trying to decide if it was okay to leave when the door finally opened.

A woman appeared. She was leaning heavily on a wooden cane, but despite her obvious discomfort, she smiled warmly. "Ah, you must be Midnight. Thank you so much for coming to see me," Miss Appleby said. She had large brown eyes and long, honey-colored hair tied up at the nape of her neck. She also really was a dead ringer for the old, dim photograph in the locket. No wonder Phil had figured out who owned it.

"You're welcome. It's nice to meet you." Midnight fumbled around in her pocket for the necklace and passed it over. Miss Appleby's face quivered as she reached for it.

"Thank you, child. I thought I'd never see it again, and I know it's silly to get so sentimental, but it means a great deal to me. Anyway…" Miss Appleby paused, as if to collect herself. "Would you like to come inside for a few minutes? This silly ankle of mine makes standing difficult, but your good deed shouldn't go unrewarded. I have cookies."

Normally Midnight was a sucker for cookies, but right now, all she wanted to do was leave. However, she was too much her mom's daughter to refuse—she had been taught to always be polite.

"Of course." She forced a smile onto her face as she stepped inside. The hallway was nice, filled with colorful prints on the wall, and a large mirror that lightened the whole place up. The living room was just as fresh, with funky ornaments, flower-filled vases, and a long, white sofa dotted with bright pillows. It all kind of reminded Midnight of a department store display.

She sat down on the corner of the sofa while Miss Appleby eased herself into a bright-red wingback chair by the fireplace.

"Ah, that's better." Miss Appleby put the wooden cane down and lifted up two knitting needles that were attached to a long trail of amber-colored knitting. "I like to make blankets for the newborn babies at the hospital."

"I see," Midnight said, trying not to think of the time

she'd tried to knit a beanie and it had ended up resembling a potato sack. She squirmed on the sofa and wondered how long she needed to stay.

"So, you have a very unique name, Midnight," Miss Appleby said, the needles making a soft clicking noise as she spoke. "I have to ask, were you named that for a particular reason?"

Midnight's cheeks heated, almost feeling Miss Appleby's penetrating gaze upon her. "Uh...yeah. I was born at midnight. On Halloween."

"Well, I'll be." Miss Appleby stopped knitting and let out a soft gasp. "So it's true."

"What's true?" Midnight said in surprise, since this wasn't how people normally reacted.

"That we share a birthday." Miss Appleby gave her a warm smile. "When I heard your unusual name, it did make me wonder. You see, I don't often come across anyone born at the exact same time I was. A nurse once told me some women try and avoid giving birth on the thirty-first of October because they think it will be bad luck."

"It's worse luck when your mom decides to give you a

name like mine," Midnight said candidly, which caused Miss Appleby to laugh.

"Good point. I got teased enough for having a birthday on such a well-known day, but I imagine that you must get even more considering your name. Let me guess. They call you freak? Ghoul? Witch?"

"Yes." Midnight nodded, years of taunting coming back to her. Normally she tried to forget about it, but meeting someone else who'd been through it was almost a relief.

"And then there were the birthday parties." Miss Appleby let out a soft sigh. "All I ever wanted was a pink cake, but all I got was—"

"Something black and in the shape of a coffin or cauldron?" Midnight finished, trying not to think about all the years of having to act happy about her birthday.

"That's about the sum of it. Still, being born at this time also has its advantages." Miss Appleby gave Midnight a considering look. "In fact…I'm in desperate need of some help, and my helper needs to have been born precisely at midnight on Halloween. Would you like a job?"

Midnight let out a startled gasp. "How did you know that I was looking for a job? Did Phil tell you?"

"No, he didn't mention a thing," Miss Appleby assured her, a hopeful gleam in her eyes. "But does this mean you do want a job?"

"I do." She nodded, bowled over by her good luck. While Midnight believed in planning, her mom believed in positive thinking. Perhaps Mom was right… "So what kind of job is it? Running errands and sorting out your yarn? Because I'd be more than happy to do either of those things. Oh, and my mom taught me to cook. I'm not very good at it, but I can boil an egg. And—"

"Actually," Miss Appleby cut in, leaning forward, "I had something a bit different in mind. I was hoping that you could help me hunt ghosts."

Chapter Four

"Wait. *What?*"

"I know it seems ridiculous." Miss Appleby gave her a rueful smile. "Because let's face it: when people think of a ghost hunter, they don't automatically conjure up a middle-aged lady with a broken ankle and a passion for knitting."

"Okay." Midnight sucked in a deep breath and waited for the punch line, but it didn't come. "But you don't mean *ghost* ghosts, do you?"

"Unfortunately, I do." Miss Appleby's needles continued to clink together in a soft chorus. "Though if we're being technical, the correct term is spectral energy."

"Spectral energy?" Midnight echoed.

Miss Appleby nodded. "Only people born when the veil between the worlds is at its lowest can even see spectral energy. And if you can't see it, you can't stop it, which is why I need your help. At least until my ankle's better. The doctor says it might take two to three months."

Midnight was sure she could feel her pulse flutter. One moment, they were having a perfectly nice conversation, and the next moment, they were talking about ghosts.

"I think there's been some mistake." Midnight got to her feet and tried to ignore the goose bumps puckered up along her arms. "I can't see ghosts or spectral energy or whatever you want to call it. I think I'd know if I could."

"Would you?" Miss Appleby's brown eyes carefully studied Midnight's face. "When most people think of ghosts, they think of what they've seen in the movies, but the truth is far different."

"Different how?" Midnight asked, unable to help her curiosity.

"When someone dies, they leave behind an essence.

In theory, their essence is meant to pass across to the Afterglow, but something different happens in Berry. There's a phenomenon called a Black Stream—a huge ripple of electromagnetic currents that encircles our entire town and sucks spectral energy into inanimate objects. People's energy gets stuck here, and when spectral energy stays in an inanimate object for too long, it festers and turns into something evil and endangers our whole town."

Midnight frowned. "How do you know all this?"

"Because I see it, Midnight—flickering white lights, a strange buzzing noise that sounds like a swarm of bees. Of course most people don't notice it, but we're not most people. And I imagine you started hearing it when you first moved to Berry and it's gotten worse since you turned twelve years old last week."

Midnight sat back down on the sofa, her legs as heavy as lead as she tried to ignore the way her hands were shaking.

All the noises she'd been hearing.

The ones she'd been trying to ignore.

And it had been worse since her birthday.

Especially at the dance.

"What does turning twelve have to do with it?" she asked, looking over to where Miss Appleby was still sitting in the red chair.

"Because that's when our sight starts to develop. Of course, you can't see full spectral energy without your glasses." Miss Appleby finally put down her knitting. "Don't worry. I'm not a mind reader. I just know that anyone with our special talents is born with dry eyes, which means that we can't wear contact lenses."

Okay. Enough. This was crazy. Wasn't it?

Midnight didn't want to be rude, but there was no way she could continue this conversation. The worst thing was that for a moment, she'd really thought that Miss Appleby understood what it was like to be considered weird just because of when you were born. Yet now she was trying to suggest that Midnight was weird.

Well, she wasn't. And she had her friendship with Sav and Lucy to prove it. Besides, everyone knew that flicking white lights and a strange buzzing noise did not a ghost make.

"There must be someone else who can help you,"

Midnight insisted.

Someone who wasn't twelve years old.

Someone who wasn't her.

"If there is, I haven't met them." Miss Appleby looked away, her face twisted with pain. "In fact, I'd long ago given up hope of ever finding anyone who could help. I know this sounds crazy—impossible even, but I wouldn't ask you if I had any other alternative. I'm the only person who keeps Berry safe from this energy, and I'm having trouble doing it with my broken ankle."

Midnight shook her head, beads of sweat forming on her forehead.

Besides, how did she even know that Miss Appleby was telling her the truth? It was too much. She had to get out of there. Away from Miss Appleby's large brown eyes and pleading voice. She forced back the gnawing nausea in her stomach and got to her feet.

"I'm sorry. I can't help you," she said.

Instead of getting angry, Miss Appleby just let out a resigned sigh, her face gray and strained. "It's okay. Believe it or not, I do understand. Perhaps if I had my life to do over, I would've chosen differently too. But if you change your mind, please, call me. My job offer still stands."

"Okay," Midnight said, leaving Miss Appleby's house as quickly as she could.

It wasn't until she was a few blocks away that she dared to stop and catch her breath.

Living with a hippie mom and a pain-in-the-butt sister meant that Midnight had had her fair share of strange conversations, but nothing had even come close to that one. Not even when her mom had told her she was going to marry a Viking.

Spectral energy? Was it even possible?

She remembered Miss Appleby said that, without her glasses, it was impossible to see spectral energy. Midnight's panic eased up. If that was the case, then it was simple. She wouldn't wear her glasses anymore. Sure, seeing the whiteboard, objects, and people might be a problem, but failing a couple of exams and getting the occasional bruise from walking into something sure beat the alternative.

Midnight took a deep breath as she walked to Tabitha's. The sooner she forgot about what had just happened, the better.

CHAPTER FIVE

When Midnight moved to Berry, the first things she'd noticed were the trees—oaks, willows, maples, all lining the streets, flanking the winding river, and even lending their name to just about everything from her middle school to the outlet mall on the other side of town. Of course, the downside of trees was that in fall, there were a lot of leaves. Midnight kicked her way through small mountains of burnt orange, bright red, and muddy-brown foliage until she reached the address Tabitha had given her. She arrived and looked up at the huge brick wall and steel gate, which partially concealed a modern glass house.

If Midnight hadn't already triple-checked the address, she would've wondered if she had the right place. It seemed so weird that antisocial Tabitha would live in such an ostentatious home.

"I see we have the same taste," Tabitha said, coming to the front gate. Her sullen frown turned slightly upward into just a hint of a smile, though she was still wearing the black clothing she usually wore, and she was pale and lank-haired as always.

"What?" Midnight gave herself a small shake to try and clear her head.

"That look on your face when you saw the house." Tabitha waved her arm for Midnight to follow her past the ornamental Japanese garden toward the front door. "I think it's pretty gross too."

"Oh, no. I'm just surprised, is all." Midnight paused and bit down on her lip. "Do you really not like this house?"

"Not even a little bit." Tabitha shook her head, her black hair whipping around like a static halo. "It's just so sterile. So empty. So soulless."

33

"Right." Midnight nodded cautiously as she trailed after Tabitha. They walked through a state-of-the-art kitchen with a see-through dining table. Outside, a plethora of long black leather lounges faced a large swimming pool. It wasn't like Midnight hadn't been in nice houses before. Both Sav and Lucy lived in big houses too. She'd just assumed that Tabitha's house would be a lot less...bright.

Not that it mattered. All that mattered was that she could get through the rest of the day without thinking about anything that had just happened to her.

She followed Tabitha to her room. Unlike the sleek glass and chrome of the rest of the house, the walls were covered in posters of old vampire movies and bands whose names Midnight didn't recognize. However, there was also a long white desk that ran the length of the wall with a sleek MacBook Air in the middle.

"So, our project has to be about someone who once lived in our community and I have a great idea." Tabitha sat down and inspected her chipped, black nail polish while Midnight turned on her own laptop. "Everyone in the class will be doing something boring, like the history of our town's founding fathers, which is easy information to find. But I thought we could choose a random person and research their life. I have a plan of the cemetery to help us make our decision."

"Wait." Midnight looked up from her laptop. "Did you say you have a plan of the cemetery?"

"Sure did." Tabitha folded her arms defiantly. "There's nothing wrong with spending time in the hallowed, sacred grounds of our community, learning to appreciate those who have gone on to new and unknown places. Do you have a problem with that?"

Apart from being seen there? No, none at all.

But if she argued with Tabitha, it would take even longer to get the project done. Between her unsettling conversation with Miss Appleby and the fact that she still hadn't found a job, all Midnight wanted was to get this project finished and tick it off her list.

"Of course not," she said in a bright voice. "So, let's look at this plan."

"Thought you'd never ask." Tabitha grinned. She pushed aside her MacBook and unrolled a large piece of paper with small black rectangles dotted along it.

Midnight had a bad feeling that they represented dead people. This was so not her idea of a good time. "Okay, this is the cemetery. Just let me bring up the app that has a list of everyone's names."

"There's an app for Berry Cemetery?" Midnight blinked, not sure if the day could get any weirder.

"There's an app for everything," Tabitha responded, with the kind of pitying look that Midnight and Taylor normally gave their mom when she was trying to send an email.

Midnight's face heated. "Sorry. I guess it never occurred to me to look for one."

"No big deal. Cemeteries aren't your thing, so why would you look for one? Now we just need to pick someone. Any preferences? Sarah Newton? Rodger Travis? Or if you don't care who we pick, we could do Tobias Benson. His gravestone says, 'Death is sure.' Isn't that awesome?"

"Totally." Midnight crossed her fingers, wondering if it was going to get easier working with Tabitha. "So, Tobias Benson it is."

"Great. So, now we need to figure out a plan of

attack, like what days we should meet and how long it will take." Tabitha still had her arms folded, but her shoulders had relaxed.

"I can help there. I've already made up a preliminary timetable," Midnight said, relieved to be moving back to familiar territory. She brought up her spreadsheet on her laptop and turned the screen so that Tabitha could see it.

"And I thought that I was the weird one." Tabitha lifted an eyebrow. "Is this your idea of fun?"

"Of course not," Midnight said, before realizing that it was only because Tabitha was weird that she'd shown her the spreadsheet in the first place. She didn't worry about what Tabitha thought. "I just find that the more organized I am, the more time I have to relax. It's a win-win."

"R-ight." Tabitha nodded as she continued to inspect the screen. "What's with all the colors?"

"So we can easily see our schedule," Midnight explained. "I've broken down our time after school to help us plan. Red is for eating dinner. Green is for YouTube downtime, and orange is for any after-school activities we might have. Speaking of which, is there anything you'd like to schedule in?"

"You mean apart from hanging out at the cemetery?" Tabitha raised an eyebrow before shaking her head. "No. My mom's desperate for me to play tennis, but I think she's beginning to accept that I'm not country club material."

"Okay. So…No after-school activities apart from cemetery visiting," Midnight confirmed as she typed it into the cell. That was a sentence that you didn't see every day. "And nothing in the mornings?"

"Nothing but annoying my parents with my biting wit." Tabitha grinned. "What's pink for? I don't know if I'm comfortable being involved in activities associated with the color pink."

"Don't worry. It won't bite. It's just there for when I get my part-time job."

"You're going to get a job?" Tabitha looked at her with interest before reaching over and clicking on the spreadsheet cell where Midnight had written: Get a job so that I can go on the ski trip of a lifetime and make all of my dreams come true. "Ah, now I get it. You've been invited on Savannah Hanson's annual ski trip."

"How do you know about that?" Midnight gasped.

After Sav invited her, Lucy had explained that only two lucky friends received the golden invitation each year. She realized that Tabitha was staring at her. "Sorry. That was rude."

"Forget it." Tabitha shrugged. "Back in fourth grade, Sav and I were best friends."

"Are you serious?" Midnight yelped before stopping herself. If she'd been rude before, now she was being downright insulting. "What I mean is that you guys are so—"

"Different? Yeah, tell me about it. Anyway, that's all in the past."

"But what happened?" Midnight persisted, both fascinated and shocked at the idea that Tabitha Wilson and Savannah Hanson had ever shared a conversation.

"Well, let's see. I developed a taste for skulls and wearing black, and she developed a taste for ignoring me. But honestly, it's no big deal."

"O-of course not," Midnight stammered while trying not to show how sorry she felt for Tabitha. Because despite Tabitha's indifference, Midnight couldn't imagine anyone being pleased at losing Sav's friendship.

It must've been like being shown the sun and then having it taken away.

She looked around the dark bedroom and then at Tabitha's habitual smirk and realized that it wasn't just an example of what could happen if you lost the friendship of the coolest girl in school.

It was actually a cautionary tale.

CHAPTER SIX

Midnight tried to fight back a yawn on Monday afternoon as she waited at the school library for Sav and Lucy
to arrive. The final bell had rung ten minutes ago, but
at least this time she knew her friends weren't going to
stand her up. Sav and Lucy were meeting with the drama
teacher about the talent show, and then they were all
going to their favorite juice bar. Even better, Midnight
wasn't wearing a mouse costume.

On the downside, Midnight's job hunting wasn't going
well, and she'd quickly discovered that there wasn't much
call for a twelve-year-old girl with excellent spreadsheet

abilities and bad eyesight, and right now all she had on her list was crowdfunding or…

No.

She pushed the thought from her mind.

Working for Miss Appleby wasn't an option.

After all, what was the point of trying to fit in with her friends if she did something crazy like fighting spectral energy? That was the other thing. In between her job hunting, Midnight had spent hours on the Internet trying to see if a single word of what Miss Appleby had told her was true. But she hadn't been able to find one credible reference to spectral energy. In fact, all that her search had resulted in was a bunch of gimmicky ghost-hunting apps, which all promised to help find specters using electromagnetic energy. Not that Midnight believed they worked (or even knew what electromagnetic energy was), but it did prove Tabitha had been right. There really was an app for everything.

Oh no. Midnight froze as she caught sight of Logan Johnson talking to Tyson Carl at the other end of the library. He seemed too busy avoiding the spittle from Tyson's overbite to see Midnight, which gave her time to scuttle behind one of the stacks. Sav no longer had a crush on him, but Midnight didn't want to mess anything up with her friends.

She put on her glasses and Logan immediately came into focus. His dark hair was pushed back from his forehead and his deep brown eyes were narrow with worry, as he and Tyson walked to the science section, no doubt to study for the upcoming quiz. It also meant that Midnight was stuck where she was.

She crouched down and tried to ignore the way her jeans dug into her stomach. Sav and Lucy's favorite mantra was "fashion before comfort," but secretly Midnight wished that jeans could be cute and easy to move in at the same time. She sucked in her stomach. Hopefully Logan wouldn't take too long to... *Who put modern art in the history section?*

Midnight pulled it out and placed it on the floor before noticing a Judy Blume book. She took that out too, and soon she discovered at least twenty more incorrectly shelved books.

She frowned. Libraries had always been her happy place. They represented order and certainty. They had a system that could be relied on. They were somewhere that couldn't be hit with random events like your father getting killed in a car accident. Or like your mom deciding to get remarried to a Viking.

"Do you care to explain this mess?" a low voice hissed and she looked up to see Mrs. Crown, the bad-tempered librarian, looming above her. Midnight gulped and cautiously checked that Logan wasn't still around before reluctantly getting to her feet.

"They're all misplaced books that have been dumped here. Kids are so annoying," she said.

"Aren't they just," Mrs. Crown said in a brutally dry voice. "Now put these on the return cart and then get out of my library. I don't want to see you back in here for two weeks."

"Two weeks? But—" Midnight started to protest, but quickly did as she was told and scurried outside. However, before she had a chance to brood, a small flicker of light danced around the nearby flagpole and the familiar buzz jangled her ears.

Midnight pressed her lips together, much the same way she did when she wanted to ignore Taylor. She didn't care how much spectral energy she saw, as long as she didn't put on her glasses, she could pretend it wasn't there. The lights increased and Midnight resolutely turned the other way. *See, that wasn't so hard.*

A couple of minutes later, Sav and Lucy appeared, their arms linked at the elbows and their heads bobbing together as they giggled over something. As always, they looked like they'd stepped out of a clothing catalog. Midnight beamed with pride as several kids turned to stare at them.

"You're never going to believe what just happened." Sav grinned, seemingly oblivious to the attention she was generating. Then she paused and smoothed down the collar of Midnight's shirt and tweaked her hair band before giving a critical nod of her head. "Goodness knows what you'd do without me. There. That's better."

"Thanks," Midnight said. Normally she didn't like people getting into her personal space, but Sav was super touchy and loved making sure that everyone around her was putting their best foot forward. Or, in Midnight's case, her best Vans forward. Either way, she was grateful. "So, what were you going to tell me?"

"When we were talking to Miss Gregory, Lucy was drinking a can of diet soda and then she started laughing so hard that it almost came out her nose," Sav explained as they headed for the café a few blocks from the school. Midnight continued to ignore the flickering lights. It was a lot easier to do when she was with her friends.

"In my defense, I only started to laugh because you were talking in that dorky English accent of yours," Lucy retorted.

"What do you jolly well mean, old chum?" Sav protested in her fake accent. They continued to joke all the way to the juice bar. Midnight tried for the hundredth time to imagine Sav ever being friends with Tabitha. But it was impossible because Sav, with her long blond hair, great clothing, and killer sense of humor, was just so far removed from Tabitha's morbid personality. Midnight blinked as she realized that Lucy was asking her what she'd been doing.

"Nothing much," she quickly said. Somehow she didn't think that "hiding from Logan" or "ignoring spectral energy" would be an appropriate answer. "But tell me more about the talent show. Are you both entering?"

"I'm just doing some backup dancing," Lucy said. "But Sav has a solo."

"Yes, and I'm petrified after what happened last year." Sav gave a nervous shudder.

"You were robbed," Lucy immediately piped in, and Midnight nodded her head in agreement. She hadn't been at school last year but had heard about how Sav's backup vocal track had stopped working and the judges had wrongly thought she'd been singing flat.

"You can't let something like that stop you from shining," Midnight said, for once quoting her mom. "You're an amazing singer."

"Thanks, Midnight." Sav gave her a watery sniff. They reached the juice bar, snagged their favorite table, and ordered their juices.

"Okay," Lucy said as soon as they were all sucking on their cranberry zingers. "So, Sav and I have been working out a list of everything that we need to get when we go to the mall next Saturday. And, Midnight, you'll be pleased to see that we've used a spreadsheet."

"Nice job," Midnight said as Lucy produced her tablet. Though she was happy that her friends were finally embracing the power of order, she was a bit alarmed to see how long the list was. She gulped at one of the entries. "Three new swimsuits? I thought we were going skiing."

"Of course we are, but don't forget the hot tub at the end of the day," Sav explained before rubbing her chin. "Though Midnight's right. Three might be excessive. I'm sure we could get away with just two. And speaking of new, I saw the most adorable ski pants that I absolutely have to buy."

Midnight's throat tightened as the reality of the ski trip hit home. If she didn't get a job soon, she wouldn't be able to afford a pair of gloves, let alone everything else on Lucy's list. Which meant she'd have to stay home. And what if she couldn't avoid Logan the next time she saw him? Or if word got out that she went to the cemetery with Tabitha? Her friendship with Sav and Lucy would be over and she'd be forced to go back to her old life. The one where she was all alone. Unless—

The flickering lights and low buzz that had been following her since school continued in her ear, but this time, instead of ignoring them, Midnight took in a deep breath as a realization churned in her stomach.

The job with Miss Appleby. If her friends found out about it, they'd think she was a freak, but if she didn't take it, she'd be left home, and the damage to their friendship would be irreparable.

She had no choice. She had to take it.

CHAPTER SEVEN

"I'm so pleased that you changed your mind." Miss Appleby was sitting in the red chair with her walking stick close by when Midnight walked in the room. The long trail of amber knitting in her lap caught a glint of afternoon sunshine, turning it golden.

"Thank you for being so understanding," Midnight said as she studied her hands to stop herself from freaking out. After all, it was one thing to agree to take the job. It was another thing entirely to be sitting back in Miss Appleby's living room to discuss ghosts.

"Nonsense. I know better than anyone what I'm

asking you to do. I'm just grateful that you're here." The knitting needles softly clicked away in the background. "The people of Berry will never know what you've done for them, but you'll always have my gratitude."

"Er, thanks." Midnight caught her breath.

"Plus, of course, the cookies." Miss Appleby gave her a warm smile and nodded to a side table that was laden with cookies, cupcakes, two cans of soda, and a pot of tea. "We can't forget the cookies."

"Where did you get this?" Her eyes widened at all the refined sugar. Considering her mom's idea of a treat was a handful of dried cranberries, Midnight could get used to this.

"I hired someone to tidy the house and prepare my meals until my ankle's healed. Plus, what we do takes energy. A lot of energy. Why don't you pour me a cup of tea and get yourself whatever you want, and then I can start answering some of your questions. I imagine you have a long list."

"How did you guess?" Midnight poured the tea and helped herself to a large chocolate cupcake.

"Because I think we're more alike than you realize,

and if it were me, I'd want to understand exactly how it all works." Miss Appleby put down her knitting and stirred her tea. "So, what's at the top of the list?"

"I still don't understand how we're meant to stop this spectral energy." Midnight sat back down on the white sofa, making sure that she didn't spill any crumbs on it.

"What I do is hunt down and neutralize any inanimate objects that contain spectral energy. That's actually what I was doing when I dropped my necklace at your school. I was neutralizing a large green vase that sits on the school secretary's desk."

"That was you?" Midnight gasped.

Bwwrrrrrrrrrring.

Midnight stiffened as the piercing sound of a siren echoed through the room. Miss Appleby looked annoyed.

"Is that a fire alarm? Should I call someone? Do we need to evacuate?" Midnight tried not to panic.

"Unfortunately, there's no one to call." Miss Appleby awkwardly got to her feet. "That's the electroscope letting us know we've got trouble. I guess it's true what they say: there's no rest for the wicked."

"What do you mean?" Midnight's palms prickled

with sweat.

"I mean that we're about to trap some spectral energy. I'm going to need a hand with walking."

"O-of course." Midnight obediently helped Miss Appleby out the door. "Where to?"

"Down the end of the hallway," Miss Appleby instructed, leaning on Midnight's arm, her teeth gritted in frustration. She obviously hated having to rely on people, which was something Midnight could definitely relate to. It was slow going, but they finally reached a plain white wall and Miss Appleby pushed aside a large watercolor painting to reveal a hidden latch.

Midnight gasped as the whole wall slid away, revealing a hidden room. The air was colder, and she hugged her arms to her body as she stepped inside and looked around.

Unlike the rest of the house, which was modern, light, and breezy, this room was full of oak paneling, heavy oil paintings, and an overpowering bookcase that lined one wall. Along the second wall was a huge collection of bottles, lampshades, and toys, all standing side by side in random order. Her heart pounded. In the middle of the room was a large table that was covered with a glass dome, and the alarm seemed to be coming from it.

Bwwrrrrrrrrrring.

Midnight jumped as the sound vibrated through her body. "Did that get louder?"

"Yes, and it will continue to do so until the spectral energy has been neutralized. Thankfully, the house is soundproofed, so the neighbors can't hear it," Miss Appleby said. "Now, if you could go to the table and tell me where the brass arm is pointing, then we'll know where to go. It isn't always exact, but it's a good place to start."

Midnight wanted to protest. She wasn't ready to start. She still had so many questions—a whole neatly written list of them. But, as her heart continued to pound from the wailing siren, she swallowed them down.

If she wanted to go skiing, this was what she had to do.

She walked over to the table. A three-dimensional map of Berry spread across it, and above the map was a long brass arm that consisted of a series of brass cogs and wheels. It looked like the weirdest science fair invention she'd ever seen.

"What is it?" she asked.

"A flying arm electroscope." Miss Appleby eased herself into a nearby chair and glanced at the clock on the wall. Her face tightened. "It searches for spikes in the electromagnetic field and marks it on the map. That's how I know where the spectral energy will be. Can you tell me where it's pointing?"

"Okay." Midnight moved closer to the map and realized that the brass arm was hovering over a large plot on Goodison Street. "Hey, that's Humber's toy store. Are you saying that it might be in a toy?"

"Unfortunately, we have no way of knowing until we get there. Now, if you could go to the closet and lift out the smallest camera from the top shelf."

Midnight obediently went over to a large, freestanding closet in the far corner and pulled back the thick door. As she did so, the enormity of what she'd agreed to hit her in the chest.

The spectral energy could be in anything.

Anywhere.

At any time. Then she remembered Miss Appleby had been at the school on Friday night.

"What happens if the spectral energy's somewhere that you can't get to?"

"Ah. Smart girl. I like the way your mind works." Miss Appleby nodded her head in approval. "Do you see the large lenses on those cameras? It allows us to trap energy even if there's a wall between us. It also helps that I have the advantage of age and respectability. People see what they want to see. In fact, the closest I've ever come to getting caught was on Friday night. By you."

"I hope I have the same luck," Midnight said as she turned back to the closet. A dusty smell invaded her nose and made her sneeze as she stared at shelf after shelf of gleaming brass and copper cameras, all complete with huge, mushroom-shaped metal flashes.

"Technically, they're not really cameras. They're called spectral transformers." Miss Appleby nodded at the top shelf, and Midnight reached up to grab the one in question. Up close, she could see that while it looked like a camera, it was so much more. It had a copper body with a small brass canister running up one side that connected to the flash, and a brass zoom lens that poked out like a metallic beak, covered with screws and cogs. It also felt like it was made out of concrete, and her shoulders sagged from the weight.

"They get even heavier once the spectral energy becomes trapped. We use glass plates inside the transformers to trap the energy," Miss Appleby added, once again seeming to read Midnight's mind. "And speaking of glass plates. You'll need to get one from that shelf."

"Okay." She tried not to notice how much her hand was shaking as she put down the transformer and retrieved the plate in question. It was about three inches high and set in a polished wooden frame with clear glass in the middle. Once she had it, Miss Appleby directed Midnight to pack everything into a red shopping cart and announced it was time to leave.

"Are you coming with me?" Midnight asked.

"Of course. I need to show you the ropes, but once you get the hang out of it, you'll probably find it easier not to be slowed down," Miss Appleby explained as Midnight shut the lid on the cart. Whenever she'd seen people with these carts, she'd always assumed they were only carrying their groceries. Now she wasn't so sure.

"Thank you." Midnight didn't know whether to be

terrified at what they were about to do or grateful that she wasn't doing it alone. Then the alarm rang out again. The screech echoed in Midnight's ears, and without another word, they made their way outside to wait for a taxi to take them directly to the spectral energy.

CHAPTER EIGHT

Fifteen minutes later, they were standing outside Humber's Toy Emporium. Late-afternoon sun sent long shadows onto the pavement as a crowd of shoppers milled around. All in all, it seemed like a regular Tuesday in Berry, and for a moment, Midnight wondered if the electroscope had made a mistake.

Was that possible?

Then she looked up and saw flashes of pale light dancing around the building. That answered that question.

"You'll need to put your glasses on," Miss Appleby said. Out of habit, Midnight peered around to check that no one she knew was there before she slipped them over her nose. As soon as she did, a strangled gasp escaped her lips. The pale lights had been replaced by thick black clouds of pulsating energy, covering the entire store.

"It's everywhere." Her skin crawled as a family walked through the front entrance. "Shouldn't we stop them from going inside?"

"It's not that simple. How do you make people believe something that they can't see with their own eyes?"

"Yes, but we have to do something."

"And we will," Miss Appleby said before softening her voice. "I'm not being heartless. I'm just working from experience. When I first started, I did warn a family. I figured that they had the right to know the truth. Unfortunately, they thought I was crazy and called the police. I learned not to make the same mistake again. Do you understand?"

Midnight, her knuckles white as she clutched the cart, nodded numbly and silently followed Miss Appleby into the toy store.

The clerks were wearing red-and-black-striped aprons and looked harassed as their young after-school shoppers ran around with frenetic energy. A collection of old toys and memorabilia filled the walls behind the counter.

"Should I go and look around?" Midnight asked.

Miss Appleby gave a grateful smile. "If you would, dear. And remember, we want to protect all of these people—not just from the spectral energy, but also from the truth. Okay?"

"Yes." Midnight's throat tightened as she walked down one of the aisles, wishing she hadn't chosen today to wear the bright-orange jeans Sav had talked her into buying. Not only did they make her stand out, but they were also so tight that any kind of bending was difficult. She tried not to notice the way they pinched as she carefully scanned shelf after shelf.

The familiar low hum rang in her ears. Her breathing increased, and again she considered just walking away. After all, what was the point of earning enough money to go on a ski trip if she had to scare herself senseless to do it? But despite her pounding heart, she knew that she couldn't leave.

Her mom always said that once you knew the truth, you couldn't unknow it. Of course she was referring to a section of Amazon rain forest that was being illegally logged, but Midnight was sure that the same thing applied to this.

Spectral energy was out there, and it was too late to pretend it wasn't.

Midnight followed the buzzing noise until she found a swirling, angry mass of black fog. It was clumped around an innocuous display of baseball bats, pulsating like a heart. And right in the middle was a young boy with golden curls, who was just about to reach down and pick up one of the bats.

"No." She let out a strangled gasp and would've run straight toward him if a strong hand hadn't held her back.

"Remember what I told you." Miss Appleby was suddenly by her side. "They can't see what you see, can't feel what you feel. If you run over there now, you might ruin everything."

"But I have to warn him," Midnight insisted as the fog swirled around the young boy's head like a deadly crown. Fear hummed through her veins.

"What would you say? That there's an invisible wave of energy about to unleash insidious thoughts into his mind?" Miss Appleby leaned against the shopping cart. Her harsh words had the desired result, and Midnight sucked in a deep breath of air.

"You're right. I'm sorry. Tell me what I need to do."

"Good girl." Miss Appleby's tone was softer as she thrust some money into Midnight's hand. "I'll create a distraction while you get the bat. Pay for it as quickly as you can and meet me down the side alley."

"What?" Midnight gasped at the idea of having to touch the bat before recollecting her promise to follow what Miss Appleby said. "I mean, yes. Of course. What will you do?"

"Don't worry about me." Miss Appleby smiled, then stuck out her walking cane and sent several shelves of soft toys flying up into the air. She winked and turned toward the front of the store. The flying animals had the desired effect, and the golden-haired kid darted toward them. As soon as he was gone, Midnight dragged the shopping cart over to the display.

The spectral energy hissed in protest and a sound like swarming bees ricocheted in her ears. All of her instincts told her to run. Instead, she pushed her hand through the swirling blackness until her fingers clasped the top of the bat.

It felt like ice raced across her skin. She quickly walked to the counter and thrust the crumpled-up dollar bills toward the store clerk. The urge to drop the bat, to scream, to cry was overwhelming, but she forced it back as she waited for the girl to ring up the sale. Once it was done, Midnight thrust it into the shopping cart and raced out the door.

She blinked in the late-afternoon sunlight and pushed her way past the pedestrians until she reached the service alley. Her pulse pounded in her ears and adrenaline caught in her throat.

"Well done." Miss Appleby stepped out from behind an old dumpster. "We need to neutralize that bat as quickly as possible. Put it over there by the wall and then get the transformer out."

Midnight tentatively lifted the bat out and placed it up against the dull brickwork before she reached for the heavy equipment. The brass was cool to the touch and her hands shook with nerves. She was never going to get used to this.

"Pay careful attention." Miss Appleby's face was waxen and the veins on her neck were showing. "Aim directly at the center of the bat and slowly press down on the brass button, making sure your stance is good. The spectral energy will put up some resistance. Are you ready?"

No. Not remotely.

"Yes." Sweat beaded on her forehead and her glasses started to fog. She held the strange camera up and stared at the raging blackness that was framed in the viewfinder. Next to her, Miss Appleby shifted slightly. Midnight gritted her teeth and pressed down on the button.

The click of the flash echoed in the alley, and the whole place was illuminated with a blinding light. The spectral energy howled in protest and came hurtling toward the transformer so quickly that Midnight went flying backward, as if she'd just been caught in an elephant stampede.

Miss Appleby clicked her tongue. The spectral energy once again swirled around the baseball bat, as if mocking them. The buzzing increased. "If you go too fast, it will knock you over."

Really?

Midnight got to her feet and used her free hand to rub

her chest. Her arm and leg muscles were already aching. She wanted to cry, but she sucked in a breath of air to stop the tears from collecting.

"Try again, and this time press it down slowly," Miss Appleby urged.

"I don't—" Midnight started to say before biting her lip. Not only had her mom been making her meditate for several years, but she also often found that it was a lot easier to play her favorite game app when she was calm. She closed her eyes until a feeling of peace descended on her and then she studied the shot through the viewfinder.

"Don't forget to brace yourself."

Midnight planted her feet more firmly as she eased her finger down on the button. Once again the whole alley was flooded with an intense light, and this time the spectral energy was dragged into the lens of the transformer. Pain exploded as the camera kicked into her shoulder, but she didn't flinch. The hideous blackness continued to be sucked in.

Her arms shook as the camera turned to ice beneath her fingers. Then it was over. Midnight pushed her glasses farther into her face, to double check there was no more spectral energy, but the buzzing noise was gone. All she could see was the brick wall and a couple of pieces of trash at the end of the alleyway.

Her shoulders sagged and she turned to where Miss Appleby was leaning against her walking stick. Was it really over? Had they done it? Could they go home?

"Well done, Midnight. Now we need to clear out before anyone sees us."

"Okay." She nodded as she carefully lowered the transformer into the cart. Her hands were still shaking, but Miss Appleby's soothing voice helped calm her nerves. Once it was packed away, she glanced over to the baseball bat lying on the dirty ground. "What do we do with that?"

"Whatever we want. I don't suppose you like baseball?"

"I don't think I'll ever be able to play it again." Midnight shuddered. "Is it really okay?"

"It really is. Once the spectral energy has been neutralized, the object becomes harmless. If you don't want it, we can always return it to the store or take it with us."

"All those things in your cabinet, they all had spectral energy in them?" Midnight asked, recalling the strange collection of random objects. Then she let out a whistle. "It must be annoying having to buy so many things that you don't want."

Miss Appleby let out a short bark of laughter. "That's the least of my worries. Besides, not everything I neutralize is for sale. Sometimes, like with the vase at your school, it's just a case of me getting access to it when no one else is around. And sometimes, if the store's private enough, I just neutralize the object there. Believe me, it's hard to convince a store clerk why I need a pair of size fourteen basketball shoes."

"Does it ever get easier?" Midnight asked as she finished packing the cart. She helped Miss Appleby walk back out to the street, just as the kid with the golden hair walked out of the toy store.

"It took a while, but I always like to think of the bigger picture. Like that boy over there. You know that you saved his life, gave him a future. You should be proud."

"Really?" Midnight blinked. She hadn't thought of it like that before. Then she grinned as something else occurred to her. "If Sav and Lucy were here, they'd make us take a selfie."

"What's a selfie?" Miss Appleby looked perplexed.

"It's where you hold up your own phone or camera and take a photograph of yourself," Midnight explained, not surprised that Miss Appleby hadn't heard of them. After all, her own mom had thought they were like a wedgie when Taylor had first mentioned it.

Miss Appleby wrinkled her nose. "Call me superstitious, but after working with George's cameras, I can never bring myself to be photographed. Not to mention that I don't own a cell phone. Besides, we haven't finished the job yet. We still need to get the spectral energy home and disposed of, so it can't cause any more trouble."

"Oh." Midnight gulped. So much for thinking it was all over.

CHAPTER NINE

"This is where you dispose of it?" Midnight said an hour later, staring up at the old rainwater tank she'd seen the other day.

She wasn't quite sure what she'd been expecting, but it definitely wasn't a rusty corrugated-iron tank in Miss Appleby's backyard.

After they'd returned to the house, Miss Appleby had taken Midnight back to the hidden room and instructed her on how to separate the spectral energy from the glass plate where it was trapped. They submerged it in chemicals and transferred the energy down a glass tube, into a beaker. It had reminded Midnight more of a chemistry lesson than ghost hunting. And then, when she thought it couldn't get any weirder, Miss Appleby had told her to carry the extracted energy out to the backyard.

"I know it's not ideal. But it's the only way to make sure the energy is held somewhere that it won't hurt anyone. The tank's lined with lead and is big enough to hold as much as I need it to. Of course, the irony is that if the tank really did collect rainwater, my poor, old backyard might not be so dried out," Miss Appleby said as she glanced around.

Midnight, who'd been busy trying not to drop the glass jar, looked around and saw she was right. Unlike the rest of Berry, which seemed covered in trees, Miss Appleby's yard only had a few wizened trunks, and the short grass was brown and uninspiring. Then again, Miss Appleby had more than enough other things to worry about without adding gardening to the list.

"So, what happens now?" Midnight asked as the skin on her arm prickled. The sooner she could stop holding the spectral energy, the better.

"You need to connect it to that small tap at the bottom

of the tank. Once it clicks into place, turn the tap," Miss Appleby directed. Midnight nodded and twisted the tap. There was a howling noise as the energy was sucked up. She gritted her teeth, making sure she kept her hand steady until the bottle was empty.

Midnight caught her breath, not sure how much more spectral energy she could handle. "Is it really finished?"

"It really is." Miss Appleby nodded, some of the color returning to her face. "And I know you don't believe me, but it will get easier."

"I hope so." Midnight looked at her hand, which was still shaking. "Because even though I know it was a good thing to do, it was still kind of freaky. Is that how you first felt when you were getting trained?"

"Ah, my training." Miss Appleby gave a thoughtful look before nodding back toward the house. "Let's go back inside. There's someone I'd like you to meet."

"Meet?" Midnight frowned, but Miss Appleby had already started limping toward the house. Once they were both settled back in the lounge room—Midnight with a piece of chocolate cake and Miss Appleby with her ever-present knitting—the older woman looked up to a large oil portrait on the wall.

"Midnight Reynolds, I'd like you to meet my great-great-great-grandfather George Irongate. The man who started all of this," Miss Appleby said as Midnight studied the painting.

George Irongate was a serious-looking man with piercing blue eyes, small circular glasses, and a long handlebar moustache. He was wearing a black, old-fashioned suit and holding a leather-bound book in his hand.

"Your great-great-great-grandfather trained you? I don't understand." Midnight wrinkled her nose.

"That's because I wasn't quite as lucky as you. George wasn't with me when I first went out and caught spectral energy, nor was he with me when I mixed the chemicals or managed to put it in the lead-lined tank."

Midnight frowned. "How did he help you then?"

Miss Appleby gave her a patient smile. "You see, he shared our birthday. He was the one who discovered that the foulness is attracted to the glass plate in the camera and that it could be trapped. From the moment of his discovery, it was his lifelong obsession to collect as much spectral energy as he could and keep the people of Berry safe."

"So what happened after he died?" Midnight leaned forward. "Who looked after Berry until you came along?"

"No one. And it might have stayed that way if I hadn't been born. Thankfully, George wasn't just a scientist. He was also an optimist. In his will, he specified that the house must remain in the family and that if anyone was born on the thirty-first of October at midnight, they would be given a letter from him on their twelfth birthday. Imagine my surprise. I'd been hoping for a pony." Miss Appleby gave a faint laugh, but there was no hiding the strain in her voice. It was obviously the day that her life had changed forever.

"Didn't your parents freak out?" Midnight stared, still struggling to fathom that such a hidden world existed. "How did you keep it from them?"

"I'm an orphan. My parents died when I was an infant, and I was I was brought up by an elderly aunt. I'd never thought my circumstances fortunate, but it meant I was able to commit to my new role quite easily. The letter included directions to this hidden room and all of his notes." Miss Appleby pointed to seven matching leather-bound diaries propped up by two ornate horse-head bookends. "Everything George learned about spectral energy he left here in the hope that someone else could carry on his fight. He truly was a genius."

Midnight leaned back on the sofa. George Irongate wasn't the only genius. The fact that Miss Appleby had been single-handedly protecting Berry from spectral energy since she was twelve years old was amazing. For the first time in her life, Midnight realized that being born on such a weird night of the year wasn't actually that bad. In fact, it was kind of cool.

CHAPTER TEN

"Stop looking at me like that, you freak. And why do
you have your glasses on? You never wear your glasses."
Taylor glared at Midnight from across the table the following morning.

"So not looking at you." Midnight didn't bother to
add that she'd actually been looking at the wall just behind Taylor's head to check that the small flash of white
light she'd seen wasn't spectral energy. She'd been doing
that a lot over the last few days. Thankfully, in this in-
stance, all it had been was a rainbow of light from one of
her mom's crystals.

Another thing she'd been doing was reading George Irongate's diaries, and he said a person should always be prepared for spectral energy wherever they were.

Their mom joined them at the table with a large bowl of fruit salad. "Just because Midnight's wearing her glasses doesn't make her a freak."

"Thanks, Mom," Midnight said, trying to ignore the fact that for once Taylor was right. She was a freak. Well, not a freak, but definitely someone who could see things others couldn't. But at least she could get paid for it. And speaking of money—the amount of money Miss Appleby had given her was beyond anything she'd expected. At this rate, she might even be able to start a college fund as well, and—

"Earth to Midnight. Are you listening?" Her mom's voice cut in.

"Sorry, did you say something?" Midnight blinked, pushing all thoughts of spectral energy from her mind.

"Like you didn't hear," Taylor retorted.

"Phil wanted to know if we'd all like to go to his place for dinner, so we can discuss the costumes for Thanksgiving," her mom repeated as she picked up the cloak she'd been embroidering for the last week. She'd even dyed it by hand to make it more authentic.

"Do I have to?" Midnight's heart sank at the prospect. It was bad enough that she had to dress up like a Viking and go to a Thanksgiving dinner in two weeks' time with the Sons of a Gunnar; she didn't see why they had to have a meeting about it as well.

"At least you won't be dressed as a rodent." Taylor smirked and Midnight poked out her tongue. Her mom frowned in response.

"Midnight, you need to start making an effort."

"I am," Midnight protested. "But this is Thanksgiving. Why can't we just have turkey? There weren't even Vikings at Thanksgiving!"

"We will be having turkey," her mom corrected. "This isn't a reenactment. It's just a group of Phil's friends all getting together. Yes, we will be in costume and there will be Viking traditions, but there will be our traditions too—a compromise. Like what I want you to start doing. Plus, he's almost finished restoring the scooter for Taylor and he wants to talk paint colors," her mom said, and Midnight rolled her eyes. Another reason her sister had fallen so completely under Phil's spell was because when he'd seen their mom's ancient Vespa in the garage, he'd immediately offered to restore it to its former glory for Taylor.

"I like powder blue, though Phil's found a nice pale yellow that he thinks might look good," Taylor gushed, which didn't improve Midnight's mood.

"Fine. But don't blame me if I fail all of my subjects because I don't have time to do my homework," Midnight warned in a last-ditch effort to get out of it.

Her mom gave her a serene smile. "If you can fit in working for Miss Appleby and a ski trip, you can fit in homework and dinner at Phil's."

"Can't wait." Midnight pretended to look happy. Some parts of her life had definitely changed, but other parts were depressingly the same. Then she caught sight of the time and got to her feet. She was meeting Sav and Lucy before school. "I gotta go."

"Of course," her mom said as Midnight scooped up her backpack and made her way to school.

She headed straight for the old oak tree, but since there was no sign of Sav or Lucy, she pulled out George

Irongate's diary. Miss Appleby had insisted Midnight take all seven of the books home so she could learn as much about spectral energy as possible.

The cover was soft beneath her hands and smelled of age and dust.

December 1862

Finally I have discovered the source of the noises and lights that have plagued me for most of my life. It is a dark energy that I believe comes from spirits who cannot pass over to their eternal resting place. Ever since I received my new glasses from Dr. Robinson, I have been able to watch this evil wreak havoc on the living. However, it appears no one but I can see it. Thankfully, Father has insisted that I study the sciences, which I hope will allow me to find a way to stop this perversion of nature.

"Wow, that's a seriously old book," Lucy said and Midnight looked up with a start. "Why on earth would you be reading it?"

"Oh, it's nothing. Just part of the project Tabitha and

I are working on." Midnight quickly shut the diary, praying her cheeks weren't as red as they felt.

"You poor thing." Sav patted her arm. "It sounds like loads of work. Lucy and I are doing Jonathan Richards, one of Berry's founding fathers. There's a whole website about him, which means it's going to be super easy."

"You're both so lucky," Midnight said as they slowly walked toward the main building. She was pleased Tabitha wasn't there, since she'd no doubt be rolling her eyes—she'd accurately predicted the rest of the class would choose the founding fathers.

"I know, right?" Sav beamed as she held her phone up and flicked on a mirror app to check her teeth. When she was happy there was nothing stuck in them, she turned to Midnight. "Anyway, we were just talking about Thanksgiving. Lucy has to go to her grandmother's house, which is like three hours away."

Lucy let out a long-suffering sigh as if she'd just been forced to clean a chimney or work in a mine. "And then we have to stay the night. It's going to be so boring. No Wi-Fi or anything. What about you, Midnight? What are you doing?"

"Trust me, you don't want to know." Midnight groaned so loudly that her friends began to giggle and insisted on hearing all about it.

"You poor thing," Lucy said once Midnight had finished telling them about the Viking costume.

"I don't know." Sav stopped walking and studied Midnight's hair. "It could be kind of cute. You could put lots of little braids and beads in your hair, and if you got a purple dress, it would really make your eyes pop."

"Right." Midnight nodded, not wanting to add that her mom had showed her the sketch for the costume and it more resembled a sack than a dress. Still, she loved that Sav was trying to make her feel better about it instead of teasing her. Besides, she had no intention of taking any photographs of the dinner, so it wasn't like they'd ever see it. "I'll definitely try it."

"Good." Sav nodded before pulling a face. "It's a pity you can't come with us to the talent show rehearsal after school. You could've filmed it for us so we can study it later."

"Trust me, I'd much rather be doing that," Midnight said. Unfortunately, she'd promised Miss Appleby that she'd go over after school to practice with the spectral transformer. Still, on Saturday, they were going shopping at the mall, and for once Midnight would actually have money to buy things. It was an exhilarating thought and she was still grinning as the first bell rang.

* * *

Midnight's good mood faded as she arrived at Miss Appleby's house to discover her employer waiting for her in a taxi. Miss Appleby beckoned her over and they drove straight over to an old tire factory without an explanation.

"If you ask me, this place looks like a dump," the taxi driver said with a frown.

Midnight shivered as she took in the crumbling brick-work covered in graffiti and the broken gutters filled with weeds and bird's nests. Even without her glasses, the loud buzzing in her ear told her everything she needed to know.

"I'm afraid you might be right," Miss Appleby said as the driver helped her out of the back of the vehicle. Midnight dragged the red cart out of the cab. "But I promised my Realtor that I'd look at it as a possible investment. Would you be kind enough to come back for us in half an hour?"

"Sure." The driver shrugged as he returned to the car and drove away.

"I hate lying, but it was better than telling him the truth," Miss Appleby said, tightening her grip on her ever-present knitting bag. "Now, let's get to work. The alarm went off at eleven o'clock this morning, but because you were at school, I had to ignore it."

"Eleven? That must've been terrible." Midnight shuddered as she remembered the alarm's shriek. No wonder Miss Appleby was looking so pale.

"It wasn't ideal, but my bigger concern is that the spectral energy's had time to grow stronger. I packed one of the bigger transformers just in case. Do you think you'll be able to carry it?"

"Of course." Midnight lifted it out. The camera was larger than the one she'd been using and had a gigantic steel flash and two glass bulbs attached to the top of it. Miss Appleby hadn't been exaggerating about the weight. Midnight made a mental note to do more arm exercises.

"The bulbs will help fight any resistance that the

spectral energy might have," Miss Appleby explained, limping toward the entrance of the building. Midnight followed.

Her skin prickled as soon as she stepped inside. The large space was filled with cobwebs and old benches that had seen better days. Weeds were growing through the uneven concrete floor and light streamed in through the broken roof. The buzzing increased.

"Now, let's see what we've got," Miss Appleby said, putting on her glasses. She looked around. "Oh dear. I was afraid of this."

"Afraid of what?" Midnight put the large transformer on the ground and fumbled with her own glasses, slipping them on. Her throat tightened as the room transformed.

Gone were the cobwebs and pale beams of light. In the center of the room was an old wheelbarrow, which spewed out deadly tendrils like a fountain. The darkness was everywhere—covering the ceiling, the walls, the floor.

Panic seized her as the temperature dropped, turning her breath into a frosty trail of smoke. This was nothing like the darkness in the toy store. It was larger, stronger. Her limbs seemed to turn to lead.

There was a screeching noise, and the energy suddenly merged together in the shape of an arrow. It went flying over to Miss Appleby, covering her like a pulsating cloak.

Midnight screamed. "It's all over you! What should I do? Should I try and get it off you?"

"Definitely not. Just do what I taught you," Miss Appleby said. "Take the transformer and neutralize the wheelbarrow—" Her voice cut off, as if the spectral energy was stopping her from speaking.

"But how?" Midnight said, but there was no answer. The spectral energy continued to gather around Miss Appleby, hiding her from sight.

Midnight's body shook as she reminded herself that Miss Appleby had done this hundreds of times before— all on her own, and she probably didn't fall apart or get scared either. If she wanted to save Miss Appleby, she'd do what needed to be done.

She ignored her shaking fingers and lifted the transformer up from the ground. The cloying smell of sulfur hung in the air, and the dark tendrils slid across the floor, gathering at her ankles like icy fingers. It wanted to cover her, just like it had done to Miss Appleby.

Midnight held the camera up and stiffened her spine. She wouldn't mess this up.

Despite the frosty room, her palms sweat as she slowly pressed down on the button. The flash exploded around her, illuminating the darkness.

The energy howled and raced toward her. Midnight didn't move as the darkness swirled around her like a tornado. Next to her, still wrapped in the thick spectral energy, Miss Appleby whimpered.

The buzzing turned into a piercing cry. The windows in the old building shattered and fell to the ground, startling her. Still, Midnight held the transformer tightly. Her arms protested against the weight of the transformer, and its copper and brass parts were cold against her fingers. Just when she was certain she was going to drop it, the spectral energy was entirely sucked in and the darkness disappeared. The warehouse building was once again filled with pale shafts of daylight.

Midnight's whole body shook as she lowered the camera to the ground and tried to catch her breath. Next to her, Miss Appleby's face was pale and drawn, and she clutched her cane with a white-knuckled grip.

"Well, I must admit, I wasn't sure if you were going to manage it," Miss Appleby said, her voice shaking.

Midnight hugged her arms to her chest. "I didn't either," she admitted. While most of the blackness that had surrounded Miss Appleby was gone, there was still a faint smudge around her, reminding Midnight of the photograph in the locket that she'd found. "Are you okay? Did it—" She broke off, not quite sure what the spectral energy might have done.

Miss Appleby managed a feeble laugh. "You don't need to worry. It didn't turn me into an evil monster, though it wasn't a pleasant experience."

"Are you sure?" Midnight noticed the knitting bag had spilled out onto the dirt floor. She bent down to retrieve it, but when her fingers touched the amber yarn, a sharp shock passed through her. She whipped her fingers away. "Ouch."

"Oh, I should've warned you not to touch anything that's been so exposed to spectral energy." Miss Appleby pointed to the red cart. "There are gloves in there; it's always best to put them on first. Actually, I should've warned you about many things. I hope it didn't scare you too much," Miss Appleby said, her voice soft and reassuring. Some of the panic in Midnight's chest lessened.

"Only to the point of being a screaming mess," Midnight confessed as she retrieved the gloves so she could gather up the knitting without getting another shock. "So are you definitely okay? I mean it was all over you. It was—"

"Horrible? Soul chilling? Beyond words?" Miss Appleby said before sighing. "Because that's how it felt. Still, the important thing is that you kept your wits and neutralized the true threat. Now we need to get the glass slide safely into the brass container in my backyard."

"Okay." Midnight reluctantly carried the spectral transformer to where she'd left the red shopping cart. "D-did that happen because we couldn't come out and neutralize it as soon as possible?"

"Yes." Miss Appleby nodded as some of the color returned to her cheeks. "I guess you can see now why I was so desperate for your help."

"Well, next time we'll try and get to it sooner." Midnight looked up at the graffiti-covered brickwork, now free of spectral energy. She'd only agreed to help because of the ski trip, but discovering how brave she could be filled her with pride. Even dinner at Phil's didn't seem so bad after this.

CHAPTER ELEVEN

"Sav, you absolutely have to get it," Lucy pronounced. It was Saturday morning, and the three of them were crammed into one changing room. They'd been at Seven Oaks for two hours and Midnight was in heaven. On the downside, every single one of her muscles ached. In fact, she didn't even know that she had so many muscles. Still, the cool hundred dollars that Miss Appleby had given her more than made up for a few aches and pains.

The only frustrating thing was that she couldn't tell anyone about it—especially not her popular friends.

Sav wrinkled her nose. "Do you think the color's

okay?" She took another selfie and then scrutinized the image. "I'm not sure that yellow suits me."

"It does," Lucy and Midnight chorused. That particular shade of yellow would've made most people look like they had a liver disease, but it just made Sav glow even more brightly.

"Okay." Sav put her phone down and studied herself in the large mirror one last time, then grinned. "You've convinced me. I'm going to be the proud owner of the yellowest sweater in existence. Go me."

"Here, here!" Lucy cheered. "So, what about you, Midnight? Did you find anything?"

"Actually, I did." Midnight held up a black, army-style jacket. She loved the design, and unlike the orange jeans she'd worn on her first spectral outing, it would be a lot more practical when she went out with Miss Appleby.

"You can't have boring black." Lucy gave a firm shake of her head. "See, this is what happens when you spend too much time with Tabitha Wilson. You turn into a Goth."

"I'm not a Goth—" Midnight started to protest before she realized that Lucy was joking. "Ha-ha-ha, very funny."

"You're welcome," Lucy said before frowning again. "But why does Tabitha wear so much black? It's like she's allergic to color."

"Lucy, not everyone's blessed with good taste, like we are," Sav said seriously, though a hint of a smile tugged at her mouth.

"Yeah, but don't you think that she's just a little bit weird? It's like she wants to fade away into the background," Lucy persisted. "What do you think, Midnight? After all, you're the one who's been spending time with her."

"Just for our project," Midnight protested, not quite sure how she was meant to answer. Thankfully, before she could, Sav patted her arm.

"Lucy's only teasing. You know what she's like."

"Well, I might be teasing her about Tabitha, but I'm not teasing her about the jacket," Lucy said. "It's so boring and baggy. Why not get a white, cropped jacket? Sav got one in red last week and I have a pink one. We could all match."

White? It wasn't exactly practical, and there were no pockets for the spare glass slides that she'd need to carry when she was hunting spectral energy. Then again, there was no way Lucy could possibly know that.

"You're so right, Lucy." Sav's eyes sparkled and she darted out of the changing room. She returned several moments later with the short white jacket and gave it to Midnight. "You have to do it."

"Yes, but—" Midnight tried to protest again but her friends shouted her down, so she reluctantly slipped it on and stared at herself in the mirror. The jacket looked cool with the floral dress and leather boots she was wearing, but as her green eyes, sensible hair, and snub nose stared back at her, Midnight knew something was wrong with the picture. She just couldn't figure out what.

"It's perfect!" Sav gave a nod of approval. "And it'll look great with your blue-and-white-striped T-shirt."

"Absolutely," Lucy agreed. Her stomach rumbled, causing them all to burst out laughing. "Okay, I'm starving. How about Sav and I snag a table at the food court and you can meet us there once you've paid?"

"Sure but don't you guys have to pay for your things too?"

"Sav paid before when she went out to get that white

jacket for you," Lucy quickly explained.

"Yeah, like I told you, we're shopping experts," Sav added before shooting Lucy a wink. "Plus, we don't want to miss out on getting a good table."

"Oh, of course." Midnight nodded. She didn't go to the mall a lot, but her friends had told her how busy the food court could be. Besides, Midnight was still unsure about the white, cropped jacket and she wanted to think about it on her own. She tried to lift her arms, as if she were holding a spectral transformer, and suddenly she realized what the problem was. It was too tight and constricting. Like it was only designed to look good, not to be functional.

She wanted the black jacket, but she didn't want to risk Sav and Lucy being offended if she didn't buy the white one. She pulled out her phone and brought up the calculator. If she was careful with her money, she should just about be able to afford both. Before she could change her mind, she hurried to the counter.

She was still smiling as she left the store and headed to the food court. The marble floors shone like mirrors. The whole mall was decorated with giant gold and silver pumpkins and thick ropes of tinsel leaves, giving it a festive feeling. There was an electric zing of excitement in the air as Midnight made her way down the escalator. But her happiness was broken by a now-familiar buzzing sound.

She took a deep breath, remembering a passage from George Irongate's first diary.

> Through intensive investigations, I have discovered it is not unusual to hear and even see small amounts of spectral energy. My conclusion is that as long as it isn't attached to an inanimate object, it is quite harmless. However, I can't afford to make mistakes, so I've decided to investigate every single case.

Midnight frowned. As tempting as it was to ignore it, what if it was something serious? She knew what George Irongate would do, what Miss Appleby would do.

She checked that no one she knew was around and slipped on her glasses. The blurred masses of the food court came into focus. As always, it struck her how different the world looked when she could see it.

People were hovering around numerous food counters ordering what her mom called "reconstituted chemicals." Midnight craned her neck and peered up the escalator to the floors above, but all she could see were the long chains of tinsel glittering like icicles.

She reached for her phone. It might be nothing, but she'd better call Miss Appleby to see if the alarm had gone off. There was no answer, so she tried again, but it went unanswered as well. Midnight frowned. Now she had two problems—possible spectral energy and the worry that something might have happened to Miss Appleby.

She chewed her lip, trying to decide what she should—

"Hey, Midnight."

Logan Johnson?

Midnight gulped. She'd been so busy looking for spectral energy that she'd somehow managed to miss what was right in front of her. Or who was right in front of her.

"L-Logan," she stammered. His dark hair hung across his forehead in a tangled wave. He was also the last person in the world that Midnight wanted to see. Thankfully, Sav had now turned her attention to Finlay Gibson, but

Midnight didn't want to risk upsetting her again. "You, um, startled me."

"Sorry." He blushed. "I didn't mean to. I was trying to wave but you were a million miles away."

"Oh." Midnight made a mental note to never look for spectral energy at the mall again. She didn't care what George Irongate recommended. "I was just, er, admiring the decorations."

"Right. Well, it's cool to see you here. I didn't think the mall was your sort of place."

"What do you mean?" Midnight stiffened. Was it her outfit? What had marked her as an outsider?

"Nothing. Sorry, that came out wrong." Logan bit his lower lip. "I just meant that you have your own kind of vibe."

"Oh." She did? Midnight loosened her shoulders. She didn't really know what a vibe was, but all the same, it was cool to hear it. Then she realized he was staring at her. With his deep-brown eyes. They were nice eyes—the color of her favorite chocolate. Why had she never noticed before? Midnight's breath quickened as she found herself trapped in his gaze.

"Actually, I was wondering if you could give me some help with my science project," he said. "I still can't figure out how it all works."

"Right." Midnight studied her shoes. The organizational geek in her longed to help him, but she didn't think it was a good idea. Plus, she seemed to have an inability to form proper sentences in his presence. It was kind of a problem. "Well, I've got…you know. Stuff. Lots of it."

"I understand," he quickly said. After several more awkward seconds, he shrugged. "Okay, so I'd better go."

"Sure." Midnight's cheeks burned as he disappeared into the crowd.

She found Sav and Lucy at the far end of the food court looking at a green sweater. Midnight didn't remember seeing them buy it, but as soon as she reached them, Sav quickly thrust it back into a bag. Perhaps they'd bought it after they'd left her?

"There you are. We were starting to think you'd gotten lost," Lucy complained as Midnight slid into the booth. "And what are those horrendous things doing on your face? I thought you only wore them at school in emergencies."

"What?" Midnight yelped as she realized she still had her glasses on. She reached up to her face and pulled the offending frames off. The world promptly went blurry again and Sav gave her a sympathetic pat on the arm.

"Relax, Lucy. They don't look that bad on her," Sav said, though her voice lacked conviction. Midnight quickly put the glasses away. "So—"

"No way. Look who's here," Lucy cut in, pointing to a blurry figure. Somehow Midnight knew just who it was. Logan. Her face heated. "And can you believe what he's wearing?"

"It's a Peppa Pig T-shirt. Is he for real?" Sav said in such a loud voice that Logan looked over. Even with Midnight's hazy eyesight, it was obvious that he'd heard the conversation. Sav immediately put her hands over her mouth to show that it was an accident and Lucy burst out giggling. Logan quickly turned and walked in the other direction.

"Sav, he so heard you," Lucy admonished.

"I know. I'm so bad, but in my defense, did you see

that shirt?" Sav wrinkled her nose and gave an elaborate shudder.

"Right." Lucy gave an emphatic nod before they both looked at Midnight, waiting for her to join them in the conversation.

"Um, yeah," she mumbled before being saved by a group of boys who walked past. They immediately captured her friends' attention, and the rest of the time was spent discussing how cute they were until it was finally time to catch the bus home. Midnight tried her best to join in, but between worrying about why Miss Appleby hadn't answered her phone and hoping that Logan hadn't heard what Sav and Lucy had said about him, it was hard to concentrate. At least her friends didn't seem to notice, which was the main thing that mattered.

CHAPTER TWELVE

"So, I think we should all go back to my house and try everything on," Sav announced as their bus came to a halt in their neighborhood.

"Oh," Midnight said, feeling torn. The idea of spending more time with Sav and Lucy was tempting, but what if something had happened to Miss Appleby? She'd tried to call several more times, but there hadn't been an answer. Or worse, what if she later discovered that the spectral energy she'd heard buzzing at the mall really was dangerous? She shook her head. "Sorry, I can't go."

"Let me guess, you need to meet Tabitha Wilson?"

Lucy said as she arched her brow.

"Something like that," Midnight muttered, not sure if her friends would think it better or worse that she was ditching them for an older lady who liked to knit. She waited until Sav and Lucy had disappeared down the street, then headed to Miss Appleby's.

"Midnight. This is a surprise," Miss Appleby said, opening her door. She gestured for Midnight to come inside. "I didn't think we'd arranged to meet today. Of course my memory isn't what it once was."

"We didn't," Midnight said, suddenly wondering if it was a mistake to have been so concerned. "It's just... Well, I was at the mall and heard some spectral energy. I checked it out but couldn't see anything, so then I called and there was no answer. I guess I was worried."

They sat down in the living room. "I'm touched. It's been a long time since anyone has worried about me. I promise I'm fine. I was actually cleaning the transformers, and by the time I heard the phone, I was too late to get it," Miss Appleby said.

"I didn't know the transformers had to be cleaned. I could've done that for you."

"I didn't want to interfere with your social life," Miss Appleby said, then winced. "Well, anymore than I already am."

Midnight rubbed her brow. Of course she'd rather be with her friends, but it seemed mean not to help Miss Appleby when she obviously needed it.

"I really don't mind. And I'm here now, so you should let me clean the transformers and whatever else needs to be done," Midnight said.

A sharp beeping noise came from somewhere in the hallway, and Midnight glanced around.

"Don't worry. It's not spectral energy. It's the reminder that I need to take my pills. Now, where did I put them?" Miss Appleby began to search through the large knitting bag that was never far from her side. "I must have left them upstairs."

"Would you like me to get them?" Midnight offered.

"No," Miss Appleby said sharply. "I was having some work done on the floorboards, which was how I fell and hurt my ankle in the first place. It's incomplete and I'd hate for you to injure yourself too. I should've mentioned it sooner."

"Of course," Midnight said as she realized that underneath her employer's makeup, she was looking pulled and pale. No wonder she'd sounded so short. "Is your ankle still hurting?"

"It's not so bad," Miss Appleby said, though it was obvious that she was lying. However, her face brightened as she glanced over to the shelf. "And look, the pills were here all along. Would you be kind enough to get me some water?"

Midnight immediately obliged and was relieved when the color began to return to Miss Appleby's face.

"Thank you. That's much better." Miss Appleby resumed her knitting, the never-ending trail of amber baby blanket curled around her knees like a snake. "And now, tell me how you're coping with this secret, new job of yours. I know it can be a difficult balancing act. Do you think your mom or stepfather have noticed anything?"

"He's not my stepfather," Midnight quickly corrected before clamping down on her lower lip. Her mom always got mad when she said things like that. "Er, I mean, he's engaged to my mom but they're not married yet." Or, hopefully, ever.

"I didn't mean to upset you. I know firsthand how hard it can be to be asked to be part of a new family." Miss Appleby momentarily stopped her knitting as her brown eyes filled with sympathy.

"I'm okay," Midnight said, once again touched at how well Miss Appleby seemed to understand her. "And I don't think they have noticed anything. It's all down to time management. I like to break my day down so that nothing gets overlooked. At home, I use a spreadsheet, but I find that having a good app really helps. My current one lets me set reminders, put in notes, and it even gives me a daily affirmation."

"An app? I'm not sure I follow." Miss Appleby wrinkled her nose and it took all of Midnight's willpower not to laugh.

"They're just software programs that you can use on your phone or mobile device. You can get them for just about everything from calculators to games," Midnight explained as she flicked through her phone. She brought up the spreadsheet app so that Miss Appleby could see it. "You can get one for virtually anything."

"I'm impressed." Miss Appleby widened her eyes and

nodded her head, which made Midnight smile. Normally when people commented on her spreadsheet addiction, it was because they thought she was strange. But Miss Appleby was different. She seemed to understand and even appreciate it.

It was a nice change.

"I'd be happy to help you set one up," Midnight said. "We could put in all of your doctor's appointments and when you have your physical therapy. Then you could have another one when you're back up on your feet."

Miss Appleby looked at her fondly as she picked up her knitting. "You're so sweet, and don't think that I'm not grateful, but there really isn't much need for me to manage my time. You see, my life's pretty simple. I'm either hunting spectral energy or I'm here."

Midnight sat back down in the chair. "But you must go out and do other things. Like shopping? Seeing friends? Vacations?"

"I wish I did." Miss Appleby busied herself untangling her yarn, making it impossible to see her eyes. "But I have my food delivered to me, along with everything else I need. As for friends, unfortunately, they can be hard to maintain when you're at the whim of spectral energy."

"That's terrible." A lump formed in her throat. She knew that Miss Appleby was dedicated to what she did, but to put her entire life on hold for no recognition or reward was sad. "There must be some way around it."

"I'm afraid there isn't. As you've seen, the longer spectral energy's trapped in an object, the more powerful it becomes. Which means I need to get to it as soon as the alarm rings. And it's impossible to hear the alarm if I'm not near the house."

"Can't the electroscope be made portable, so you could take it with you?"

"If there's a way, I don't know it. Unfortunately, George Irongate's long dead. And no, don't look sad or feel sorry for me. I can assure you that I'm perfectly fine with my lot." Miss Appleby gave her a wistful smile. "Though I must confess it was one of the reasons why I hated asking for your help. I know that this can be challenging and it's not what I'd wish on anyone else. Still, as soon as I'm back on my feet, you can return to your normal life."

"But what about you? You can't return to a normal life." Midnight fidgeted with her fingers. She'd have a ski trip and her friends while Miss Appleby would be stuck in her living room, knitting and waiting for the electroscope. "Don't you miss it?"

"I try not to think about it," Miss Appleby admitted, but when she looked up, her brown eyes were clouded, as if filled by a long-lost memory. "I did love to dance. Not that I'd be much good at it now, even without a broken ankle. Still, I knew what I signed up for, so please don't feel sorry for me."

"At least let me help."

"Are you sure? It's very smelly work."

"It couldn't be worse than the onions my mom used to dye one of Phil's Viking tunics last week," Midnight assured her as they stood and made their way into the secret room.

For the next hour, Midnight learned how to take apart the transformers and painstakingly clean and polish the many parts. She also checked the chemicals that Miss Appleby used to release the spectral energy from the glass plates and polished the numerous brass cogs and levers on the flying arm electroscope.

The rancid fumes of the sulfur caught in her throat,

which she tried to ignore as she fitted the brass arm back onto the machine. As she worked, she looked up at the many portraits on the wall.

She felt like she already knew George Irongate, thanks to his diaries, but they'd been written long before he had married Mary and before his daughter, Elizabeth, was born. Midnight liked to think they were nice. They certainly looked nice. Mary had long, pale hair piled high and a wide mouth that seemed to smile at Midnight. Elizabeth looked to be around twelve, with large, doll-like eyes and a lacy, white dress that looked uncomfortable.

Thanks to the diaries, Midnight knew just what a great inventor George had been. She bet if he'd still been alive, he probably could've invented a smaller flying arm electroscope, something portable. After all, computers were once as big as a house, but now they were the size of a phone.

In fact, what they needed was an app.

Midnight gasped and pushed the electroscope to one side.

An app was exactly what they needed.

George Irongate had stated several times that he based his inventions on scientific principles he'd learned in college. What if those same principles were used in the ghost-hunting apps she'd found? Her heart pounded as she flicked through George's old, leather-bound diary until she came to the section she wanted.

I've concluded that the best way to find spectral energy is to measure the levels of electromagnetic energy. Therefore, it is my intention to build a device to help me.

Midnight grabbed her phone and started searching. Moments later, a list of ghost-hunting apps appeared. She clicked on the first one and scanned the information. It used electromagnetic energy. Her hands shook as she clicked on the next app. It was the same.

Then she grinned as she set up a new spreadsheet and got to work.

She might not be able to build an app herself, but when it came to researching, she was a wizard. Ten minutes later, she had a long list of potential apps. Now she just needed to find out if they worked. She hurried into the other room, where Miss Appleby was sitting in her red chair, knitting.

"Ah, there you are, Midnight. Let me guess, you've run out of cleaning cloths."

"Actually," Midnight said, her heart banging against her chest. "I was looking for some spectral energy."

"What?" The knitting needles in Miss Appleby's hands dropped noiselessly to her lap. "I don't understand."

"I've been looking at ghost-hunting apps and I think they're based on the same technology that George Irongate used when he built the flying arm electroscope," Midnight said, the words tumbling out.

"How can you be so sure?"

"Because it's all here in the diary." Midnight held it up. "And I've been going through all the apps, and I've found some that we can test."

"Is it really possible?" Miss Appleby's voice wasn't much above a whisper. "I might be able to have my life back? Leave the house and still do my duty?"

"I don't know," Midnight said truthfully, her phone clutched tight in her hand. "But I thought we could try them. Except to do that we'd need—"

"Spectral energy," Miss Appleby finished off.

Midnight nodded. "Yes. I mean we could wait until the alarm goes off. But it would be good to test them now. Is that possible?"

"George recommended that I keep a small amount of energy nearby. As a reminder of how important the work is. I wonder if he suspected we might need it for something like this," Miss Appleby said as she took in a deep breath and reached for the small brass box she kept on the bookshelf. "Okay. I think it's probably best if we go to the study and get a transformer set up. We don't want to release it for longer than we need to."

"Agreed." Midnight helped Miss Appleby to her feet, and they made their way back to the hidden room. Midnight collected the transformer and got it ready and then got on her phone and downloaded the first of the ghost-hunting apps. Once it was loaded, she put on her glasses. Miss Appleby slowly lifted the lid on the brass box.

Dark streaks darted out toward the ceiling and the flying arm electroscope rang out in alarm. Midnight's pulse hammered and Miss Appleby's eyes were wide with hope.

They both looked at the phone in Midnight's hand, but while the spectral energy continued to stream out and the alarm screeched in their ears, the electromagnetic meter on the screen remained undisturbed.

It hadn't worked.

Midnight swallowed hard as she put the phone down and picked up the spectral transformer. Her hands shook as she pressed down on the brass button and watched as the dark energy was dragged back toward her. Once the room was cleared and the alarm stopped its incessant noise, the pair of them sat down.

"I'm sorry. I really thought that one would have the best chance of working," Midnight said.

"But there are others?" Miss Appleby said, her mouth in a thoughtful line.

"Yes. Does that mean you're not mad? Should we try again?"

"Of course we should try again." Miss Appleby smiled at her. "After all, you've read George's diaries. It took him months to perfect the flying arm electroscope, and imagine what would've happened if he'd given up the first time it hadn't worked."

"You mean when it blew up on him?" Midnight said, recalling the diary entry in question. "I think he even burned an eyebrow."

"A small price to pay for what he has given the world." Miss Appleby got back to her feet. "So, if you're happy to keep trying, then so am I. And thank you, Midnight, for even thinking of this. I can't tell you what it means to me."

"You're welcome." Midnight picked up her phone and downloaded the next app on her list. Then she crossed her fingers. She really hoped that this one would work. For all their sakes.

Chapter Thirteen

"What's that smell?" Taylor said as she sashayed into the kitchen on Sunday morning. Midnight stiffened as she glanced down at her sneakers. She'd changed her clothes as soon as she'd arrived home to get rid of the smell but hadn't thought about her shoes.

"I was helping Miss Appleby sort out some of her old clothing, and I guess they were a bit stinky." Midnight studied her fingernails and didn't make eye contact.

"A bit?" Taylor made an exaggerated show of holding her nose.

"It was probably the mothballs," her mom said as she

lifted a tray of gluten-free brownies out from the oven.

Phil fiddled with the broken coffee machine. When he wasn't being a Viking, he seemed to spend all his spare time fixing broken appliances and painting walls. "I think it's wonderful that Midnight's giving Miss Appleby all the help she needs."

"Yeah, Taylor." Midnight grinned, resisting the urge to poke her tongue out at her sister. But she was poking her tongue out on the inside. Taylor shot her a dark look in return.

"So, how's Miss Appleby feeling?" her mom asked, ignoring their antics. "Is her ankle getting better? She must hate being trapped in the house like that."

"I think it's healing," she said.

They'd tried out fifteen apps yesterday, and they'd finally found one that seemed to work. The winner was a spoofy ghost-hunting app that looked more like a game than an electromagnetic energy reader. It even had a silly ghost cartoon that popped up and danced around when it sensed new energy.

She sighed and looked at the time. She was due to meet Tabitha to work on their history project.

"I've got to go." She stood and reached for her backpack.

"Okay, but don't forget that you'll need to be back here by three o'clock."

"What's happening at three o'clock?"

"Remember, we're all trying on our costumes for the Thanksgiving dinner? Don't tell me that you've forgotten." Her mom arched her eyebrow.

"Of course not," Midnight quickly assured her, though she had been trying to forget all about the costume she had to wear. Her mom had been sewing it all week, and there was even talk of them all brushing dirt onto their faces to make them look more authentic. Suddenly, she thought longingly to when the mouse costume was the weirdest thing in her closet. "Er, I just meant that I didn't know I had to try it on today. And now I really need to go or I'll be late."

"Would you like a lift?" Phil said, putting down his screwdriver. "I need some tools from the workshop to fix this machine. I could drop you off on the way."

"No thanks." Midnight caught her mom sending her a warning look. "I like walking."

"Yeah right," Taylor muttered under her breath, earning her a sharp glance from their mom.

"Of course." Phil gave a quick shrug. Without another word, Midnight raced out the door. Not that she was in a hurry to get to Tabitha's, but hanging out with Phil wasn't exactly her idea of a good time.

The weather was getting cooler, and Midnight could see her breath. As she walked, the last of the fall leaves formed a soggy carpet. She shivered, her new, white cropped jacket doing little to keep out the cold.

"I was wondering if you'd stand me up again," Tabitha said when Midnight arrived at her house. As usual, Tabitha was dressed all in black, with her hair pulled back with a skull and crossbones headband.

"I'm so sorry that I had to keep canceling." Midnight followed her inside.

"Yeah, well once is an accident but twice smells of avoidance," Tabitha said with a defiant sniff. "I was starting to think that your friends might not approve."

"What do my friends have to do with anything?" Midnight wrinkled her nose.

"Please. Don't tell me that they haven't made any

comments about the fact that you got stuck with me." Tabitha tapped her black-painted nails against her arm.

"Don't be silly," Midnight said quickly, not quite returning Tabitha's gaze. "I can think for myself, you know."

"Really? So why are you wearing an outfit that's identical to theirs, then?"

"It's not identical," Midnight protested, not bothering to add that Sav's jacket was red and Lucy's was pink. She had a feeling that Tabitha might not appreciate the distinction. "And the real reason I had to keep canceling was because I got a job."

Tabitha arched an eyebrow. "That was quick. I guess you can mark that down on your spreadsheet. So, what are you doing?"

You wouldn't believe me if I told you.

"Just a few chores for Miss Appleby," Midnight said instead. "She broke her ankle and can't walk much on it." She set her laptop up on the desk.

"What's she like?" Tabitha looked up with interest. "I've never met her, but I have seen her at the cemetery from time to time. I like to think that she's a witch."

"A-a witch?" Midnight spluttered. "Of course she's not a witch. She's actually really nice."

"When did I say that she wasn't nice?" Tabitha blinked, as if surprised that Midnight would think it had been an insult. She let out a disappointed sigh. "I mean how cool would it be if she were a witch and teaching you how to do loads of black magic?"

"Are you serious?"

"Of course. Unfortunately, the boring truth is that she probably just goes there to visit the Irongate mausoleum. I think she's related to George, Mary, Elizabeth, and William."

"She is," Midnight said, thinking of the numerous paintings in the hidden room. But she suspected that the real reason Miss Appleby was at the cemetery was because of spectral energy. Not that she was going to tell Tabitha that. "We should get started."

"Sure." Tabitha gave a lethargic shrug, obviously still disappointed that Miss Appleby wasn't really a witch. "So, I went to the library and got out a few things to help with our research on Tobias Benson."

"A few?" Midnight opened one of the books, which

smelled of old pages and mildew. "These look like they haven't been touched in years."

"They probably haven't, so be careful with them. They were down in the archives, but Mrs. Crown lets me go down whenever I want in return for helping her sort out the sixty boxes of paper that she bought at a recent auction." Tabitha took the book out of Midnight's hand and checked that it hadn't been damaged.

"And here I was thinking that you didn't know how to have fun," Midnight quipped before biting her lip. For some reason she'd forgotten that instead of being with Sav and Lucy, she was sitting next to a moody loner who liked witches and had a fanatical interest in all things dead. But instead of looking annoyed, Tabitha started to laugh.

"Yeah, the rumors are all true. I really am a wild one."

"Not that I'm complaining," Midnight added, suddenly remembering her own run-in with Mrs. Crown. "I'm not even allowed in the library for another week, so I couldn't have gotten any books for us."

Tabitha looked mildly impressed. "You got banned from the library? Even Trevor Mitchell didn't get banned when he covered the ceiling in spitballs."

Midnight shrugged. "I just found a whole lot of books on the wrong shelf. It was a legitimate misunderstanding."

"Sure it was." Tabitha's lips began to twitch.

"It's not funny."

"It's a little bit funny," Tabitha countered, still smiling. "Logan said that you were different."

"What?" Midnight's smile faded, and she almost dropped the book she was holding before she remembered Tabitha's warning about taking care of it. "You know Logan?"

"Kind of hard not to when he lives next door. His folks like tennis as much as mine."

"Oh," Midnight said in a neutral voice. She'd been surprised to discover that Tabitha and Sav had once been friends, but it was even stranger to imagine Tabitha and Logan hanging out.

"He's pretty cool. Sometimes he even lets me paint his fingernails black, and he helps me with science."

"Science?" Midnight's eyed widened. "That doesn't make sense. He hardly understands it himself. He doesn't even know what gravitational pull is."

Tabitha shot her a confused look. "Um, yeah he does. He's a total brainiac."

"So why would he keep asking me for help?" Midnight drew her eyebrows together.

Tabitha shrugged. "Maybe he wants to hang out with you. Why? Are you interested?"

"Of course not." Midnight gave a violent shake of her head before realizing that Tabitha was his friend and might think she was being rude. "I mean—"

"Relax. I'm not Sav and Lucy. I don't care if you like him or not. I also don't betray people behind their backs, so I'd never tell him anything you said."

"Oh. Right." Midnight winced. She wasn't sure what she felt worse about: misjudging Tabitha or saying she didn't like Logan. "Honestly, I don't know how I feel, but I do seem to lose the ability to speak English when I'm around him. I think it might be an allergy."

"I see." Tabitha's lips twitched in amusement. "So I guess we'd better get to work. Unless you want to keep talking about boys?"

"Definitely not." Midnight hid her face behind the laptop screen.

They spent the next hour researching the person who they had randomly picked to be the center of their history project. They discovered that Tobias Benson was a local lawyer who married his neighbor and had three girls. He also liked baseball and bird-watching. It was surprisingly easy to work with Tabitha. Despite her gloomy appearance, she was smart and studious.

"Okay." Midnight got to her feet. "So, should we meet here again on Sunday?"

"Can we change it to Black Friday? My folks are making me do something on Sunday. I'd like to go to the cemetery to take some photographs of Tobias's gravestone. Plus, I think I know where his parents are buried, which might be cool to mention."

"Is there any chance that if I say no to the cemetery you'll stop bugging me about it?" Midnight checked.

"Nope." Tabitha shook her head, sending her dark hair billowing out around her face. "So, what do you say?"

I say that between Miss Appleby and you, my life has become pretty strange lately.

"Fine." Midnight sighed. "The cemetery it is."

CHAPTER FOURTEEN

By the time the final school bell rang on Wednesday, Midnight was rethinking the ghost app. The good news was that each time it had gone off, it had been completely accurate. Miss Appleby had given her a spectral transformer so she could respond to notifications on her own, and she was making more money than she'd ever dreamed.

The bad news was that it kept going off, and trying to juggle everything was proving to be complicated, even with a spreadsheet. She yawned as she caught up to Sav and Lucy. They were checking their reflections in the mirror that Lucy always carried with her.

"Have you ever thought about wearing makeup?" Lucy studied Midnight's face and made a clicking noise with her tongue. "Because a little bit of foundation might do wonders for those bags under your eyes."

Midnight touched under her eyes. "What bags?"

"They're like two bruises," Lucy offered as she held the mirror up.

Midnight winced. She did have bags.

"Midnight doesn't need to wear makeup if she doesn't want to," Sav chided. She held out a tube of pale pink lip-gloss. "But you could always try this. It will detract from the shadows under your eyes and everyone knows that lip gloss isn't really makeup. It's more like a necessity."

Midnight wasn't quite sure she believed that. More to the point, neither would her mother, who'd refused to let Taylor wear even tinted moisturizer until a few months ago.

"Maybe," Midnight said in a diplomatic voice. Sav fiddled with the tiny golden studs that were sitting in her earlobes. Midnight looked at them with interest. "Are those new? I haven't seen them before."

"Oh." Sav paused for a moment before smiling. "Yeah, aren't they cute? My aunt sent them to me as a good-luck present for next week's talent show."

"And speaking of the talent show," Lucy quickly cut in, "didn't you want to go rehearse?"

"I do. You guys are coming to watch, right? You know how nervous I get." Sav gave a grateful nod of her head, not looking at all nervous.

"Definitely—" Midnight started to say before she was cut off by the sound of the ghost app going off in her school bag. "A-actually, that's probably my mom wanting me to go straight home."

"Sure." Sav's mouth tightened; then she plastered on a smile. "Well, have a great Thanksgiving. I get back on Sunday night, so I'll talk to you then."

"Absolutely," Midnight said, trying not to feel guilty that she had to cancel.

Once her friends had gone, she studied the message. The GPS map showed that it was at Butler Park, and if she walked quickly, she could get there in about fifteen minutes.

By the time she reached the park, the sky was the color

of steel and she had been hit with the low buzz that always accompanied the spectral energy. Midnight caught sight of rapid flickers of white light dancing above an ornate water fountain. She pulled out her glasses and put them on. As always, the true face of spectral energy made her gasp. The clear columns of water were replaced by layer upon layer of swirling black fog.

Midnight fought back her fear and ducked behind a neat shrub to unpack the spectral transformer. She paused to check that the glass plate was correctly loaded and that the flash was hooked up. Once it was ready, she aimed it directly at the vile energy and pressed down on the button. The flash illuminated the sky and the swirling fog howled as it was dragged into the camera. By the time it was finished, her forehead was covered in sweat from the effort. She quickly put the transformer back into her bag.

"Hey, Midnight," a voice said from behind her.

Midnight slowly swiveled around and looked up. A silent gasp escaped her lips.

Logan Johnson.

Why did this keep happening to her?

The shirt that had offended Sav and Lucy was gone, and he was wearing a pair of jeans and a blue hoodie with a robot on the front. Midnight scrambled to her feet and tried not to think about how close she'd come to being caught—or how close he was standing to her.

"What are you doing here?" she said, hoping that she didn't look as panicked as she felt.

"Kid sister. Park. Too much energy," Logan said as he nodded his head over to a little girl with long, dark pigtails, who was wearing a tutu. She was doing somersaults on the frosty grass while singing at the top of her voice. "So, how about you?"

"I just felt like some exercise," Midnight lied.

Logan's brow furrowed. "At a fountain?"

Midnight tightened her grip on her bag. "Well, um, I made a bet with my older sister that I'd run around it five times."

"Man, sisters are the worst." The confusion left his eyes and he laughed. It was a nice laugh and Midnight found herself smiling. "My sister was supposed to take Bella to the park while my parents practice with their band, but she begged me to do it just because she wanted to go shopping with a friend. What's that about?"

"It's their duty to make our lives a misery," Midnight explained, momentarily forgetting that she'd only made up the bet with Taylor to cover what she'd really been doing. In her defense, her sister had made her do more than enough dumb things in the past. "So, your parents are in a band. That's cool."

"Not everyone would agree with you. Most kids at school think it's lame."

"My mom's about to marry a guy who dresses up like a Viking and we all have to go along to a Viking Thanksgiving. I think I win lame," Midnight said.

"Oh, hey. I know those guys. They practice at the park every Saturday. It kind of looks like fun."

"I guess," Midnight said. "Though I'm not sure they do it to be fun. I think it's about preserving history. At least that's what Phil said."

"Right." Logan grinned, his dark eyes catching hers. Midnight's breath quickened. "Actually, Midnight, I was—No. Bella. Peppa does not want to explore the fountain." They turned to see his young sister dangling a vaguely familiar pig over the water.

"Sorry." Bella immediately stopped what she was doing and gave the pig a pat on the head, then resumed her somersaulting.

Logan sighed. "She's obsessed with Peppa Pig. I mean really obsessed."

Midnight let out a little gasp. "Was Bella with you last weekend when I saw you at the mall?"

"Oh yeah." He rolled his eyes. "I was kind of hoping that you hadn't noticed the shirt. They were doing a big promotion at the toy store and Bella insisted that we all had to wear our best shirts. I live in a house that's ruled by a three-year-old."

Midnight bit down hard on her lower lip, a wave of shame racing through her. "A-about at the food court. I'm not sure what you—"

"Relax, Midnight," he said, scuffing at the grass with his sneaker. "I'm not mad that Sav and Lucy were laughing. I'd probably be laughing too if I saw a twelve-year-old wearing a shirt like that."

"Oh." Midnight breathed in and caught a whiff of his shampoo. It was nice and clean smelling, not like some of the boys in her class. She tried to shake off the strange, breathless sensation as she thought about her conversation with Tabitha the other day. Was her friend right? Did Logan like her? More importantly, did she like him? Well, of course she liked him because he was nice. But did she *like him* like him?

It didn't matter. She'd told Sav and Lucy she didn't like Logan Johnson, and if she changed her mind, they'd think she'd lied to them. Which meant that no matter how cute Logan's laugh was or how dark his eyes were, she needed to stay out of his way or risk losing the friendship of the only two girls who'd ever been nice to her.

"Is everything okay?" Logan asked.

"Um, yeah. I just remembered that I've got to..." She paused. She couldn't exactly tell him she had to take the spectral transformer back to Miss Appleby's house. "Well, I've just got some things to do."

"Oh. Right." He stuffed his hands into the pockets of his jeans and nodded. "Sure. Okay, so I guess I'll see you around."

"Yeah." Midnight's cheeks burned as she turned and made her way across the park.

She was distracted by the sound of her phone and

gratefully fumbled around in her pocket and studied the pop-up message on her screen. It was from someone called Peter Gallagher. Midnight frowned. She had no idea who Peter Gallagher was and she was just about to ignore it when a familiar green ghost icon appeared on the message. Understanding dawned and she opened it up.

> Dear Ghost Hunter!
>
> Congratulations on tracking down five ghosts. We're so pleased that you love our app and would appreciate if you could take the time to complete this survey to ensure that we continue to be of service to you!
>
> Yours,
>
> Peter and the rest of the Ghost Hunting team

Midnight's lip twitched. Taylor always teased her for doing surveys and rating forms, but the organizational geek inside her could never say no to helping other people create order in their business. She followed the link. It was a reasonably simple series of questions and after hitting a lot of yes and no buttons, Midnight reached the end and was rewarded by the ghost icon doing a happy dance.

Midnight's phone buzzed again. She winced as her mom's name flashed up on the screen, reminding her that she'd promised to come home early to help with dinner. Midnight quickly sent her back an apology. First, she'd had to ditch her friends and now she'd forgotten a promise. For the most organized girl in the world, she was really having an off day.

CHAPTER FIFTEEN

The old Berry Cemetery was on a narrow wedge of land that ran halfway down a hill. Many of the long-forgotten headstones jutted out at angles, like crooked teeth. A newer, more level cemetery had been built on the other side of the river, which explained why, as Midnight pushed open the creaking wrought-iron gate the day after Thanksgiving and walked over to where Tabitha was waiting, the place was deserted.

"Hey," Midnight said as she reached her. "How are you?"

"Better than yesterday." Tabitha pulled a tragic face.

"Thanksgiving at my parents' country club? Big mistake. How about you?"

"The less said the better." Midnight shuddered, pleased it was over for another year. The highlights had been watching Phil and his friends playing rock, paper, scissors to decide who got to carve the turkey with a sword as Taylor flirted with a guy dressed up as a berserker. Oh, and in complete irony, for the first time since she'd installed the ghost app, it hadn't gone off, which was a pity because Midnight would've been more than happy to cut the festivities short.

"So bad times all around. Still, at least we're here in my happy place," Tabitha said, lifting a fancy camera from her skull-and-bones backpack. "So Tobias's grave is over on the far side. Just follow me."

"Right." Midnight blinked, not really surprised by how comfortable Tabitha was at the cemetery. Normally a place like this would've creeped Midnight out, but after everything she'd seen in the last three weeks, it was barely registering.

She followed Tabitha, careful not to trip on the uneven path. It was impossible not to feel maudlin as she passed gravestone after gravestone, but thankfully, Tabitha was more interested in getting the best camera angle than making small talk. They spent the next half hour almost in silence, taking photos of Tobias's family's graves.

They were over at his grandmother's headstone when Midnight's skin prickled. She looked up just in time to see flickers of white light radiating out from a small mausoleum. Adrenaline pumped in her veins and she thrust her glasses on. It was probably just going to be some harmless spectral energy, especially since the ghost app hadn't gone off. But all the same she knew she had to find out just in case it was—

Slender tufts of pale pink fog?

Midnight shut her eyes and then opened them again, but the delicate fog was still there, wrapped around the crumbling stonework of the mausoleum. A hundred questions surged through her mind as she watched the slim tendrils pulsate. Was it spectral energy? But if so, why wasn't it black?

She took out her phone and called Miss Appleby, but there was no answer. Indecision gnawed at her. What if it wasn't spectral energy? Then again, what else could it be? And if it was spectral energy, there really was one answer. She still had a small transformer, and if she could make her way to the other side, she should be able to neutralize it without being seen. Thankfully, Tabitha was twenty feet away, lying on the ground as she tried to get a close-up of one of the headstones. Midnight made her way toward the mausoleum.

The pink fog fluttered in answer and sent out long, thin tendrils, as if to scare her off. Midnight hardened her resolve and carefully took the spectral transformer out of her backpack. As always, the brass edges of the camera were cold in her hands as she took aim.

Before she could tighten her finger on the button, the fog disappeared.

She blinked. Miss Appleby had specifically told her that unless spectral energy was neutralized, it would grow stronger and stronger within whatever object it had taken over. In other words, it didn't just disappear. She stared at the faded stone, now purely gray. It was definitely gone. Which meant that whatever she'd just seen wasn't—

"There you are. I was starting to think I'd lost you,"

Tabitha's voice called from somewhere behind her. In one fluid motion, Midnight dropped to her knees and thrust the spectral transformer into her backpack just as Tabitha appeared.

"Sorry." Midnight tried to look casual. "I, er, was just having a look around."

"Please, I know exactly why you're here."

"You do?" Her voice was little above a croak as she wondered if Tabitha had somehow seen the pink fog—or worse, had seen Midnight with the spectral transformer. She licked her lips.

"Sure. This is the Irongate mausoleum and you're working for Miss Appleby. I figured you must want to check it out."

"This is the Irongate mausoleum?" Midnight choked.

"It is." Tabitha gave her a penetrating look before grabbing Midnight's hand. "Come on. I'll show you around."

Midnight gulped. The absolute last thing she wanted to do was look at any mausoleum, let alone one where George and his family were buried. Unfortunately, short of telling Tabitha the truth, she wasn't sure how to get out of it. When had life become so complicated?

The mausoleum was six feet deep, with three plain walls and a rusty metal gate that barred the entrance. There were no statues or carvings, like so many of the surrounding tombs had, and the only attempt to break the sparseness was the two small pillars flanking the gate.

Along the top was the name Irongate, but the engraving was so blackened with age that it was almost impossible to pick out. For all the good George Irongate had done, he and his family were fading even further into anonymity.

"Look, you can just about see the names." Tabitha pointed a finger through the rusted bars. "George Irongate was born in 1853 and died in 1895. His brother, William, is also here along with George's wife, Mary, who was born in 1857 and died in 1883, and Elizabeth was born in 1883—oh, she was born the same year her mom died. That's so sad. And even sadder, she died in 1895, just five days before her father, which means she was only—"

"Twelve years old—our age," Midnight finished as she bowed her head. Even though she'd seen the portrait of Elizabeth, Midnight hadn't known that she'd died young. And even though it had all happened such a long time ago, there was something terrible about it.

"I've often wondered why there are only four people in the crypt," Tabitha said as she took a few shots with her camera. "The cemetery didn't close until 1926, so I'm surprised that there aren't more names. Perhaps you should ask Miss Appleby next time you see her?"

And admit that she'd been snooping around the family mausoleum? Not likely. However, Tabitha was enthusiastically nodding her head, so Midnight just gave a vague reply before suggesting that, if they'd taken enough photographs, they should probably get going. Tabitha reluctantly agreed and Midnight let out a long sigh. They stepped through the wrought-iron gates and back into the normal world.

CHAPTER SIXTEEN

By Monday, Midnight was exhausted. The ghost app
had gone off three more times since her trip to the cemetery on Friday. Also, she hadn't had time to go back to
Miss Appleby's house yesterday afternoon, so she currently had a brass box with two glass slides full of spectral
energy in her backpack. Not only did it weigh a ton, but
it was also like the dark energy was creeping out into her
skin. The only good news was that while she hadn't mentioned the mausoleum to Miss Appleby, Midnight had
asked about the pink fog, and her employer had assured
her that whatever it was, it wasn't spectral energy, which

meant that was at least one thing Midnight could take off her ever-expanding to-do list.

Unfortunately, she couldn't take school off the list. She yawned as she tried to navigate the busy corridor and increased her pace as her locker came into sight.

Lucy suddenly stepped out in front of her, no sign of a smile on her mouth. "Midnight, where were you yesterday afternoon? We left you like a million messages."

"I'm so sorry," she said as Sav joined them. No smile from her either. Midnight gulped. While there hadn't been a million messages, there had been one, but she'd been so tired that she'd fallen asleep, still in her clothes, and had forgotten to send a reply. "Something came up."

"Like what?" Lucy narrowed her eyes.

Like all the work she had to do trying to make money to go on their ski trip. Yesterday, there'd been a haunted lampshade in a law office, and she'd had to get to it by standing on a trash can and aiming the spectral transformer in through an air vent. Unfortunately, she couldn't exactly tell them that. She shifted her weight and tried to pretend her bag didn't weigh more than an elephant. The sooner she got to her locker, the better.

"Um, family stuff," Midnight said instead, before realizing that Sav still hadn't spoken and that there were delicate dark bags under her normally sparkling eyes. A tingle of alarm ran through her. "Why? Is everything okay?"

"No." Lucy folded her arms in front of her chest. "Everything's not okay. It's the talent show today, and in case you've forgotten, Sav's doing a solo. Which meant she spent all of yesterday freaking out about it. We could've really used your support. You know how stressed Sav gets."

"Lucy, relax. It's fine," Sav finally said, giving Midnight a watery smile. "I know that it seems ridiculously dramatic. I was just having some last-minute nerves, which is why Lucy wanted you to be there."

"Misery loves cookie dough," Lucy said before relenting. "Sorry, I didn't mean to get in your face, but you know how nervous Sav gets before these performances. She totally needs our support."

"I'm so sorry that I forgot." A rush of embarrassment went through her. She couldn't believe that she'd let Sav down. She thought that facing spectral energy was bad, but dealing with Sav's upset face was even worse. Sav and Lucy were such good friends, and they cared enough to try and help Midnight become the best she could be. And how did she repay them? By not returning their calls. She needed to completely overhaul her spreadsheet system. She was a bad, bad friend. "How are you feeling?"

"I'm okay." Sav dabbed at the corners of her eyes and plastered on a heroic smile, but her bottom lip was trembling. "I was just being a diva."

"No you weren't," Midnight said in an impassioned voice. "Not that you need my support. You're the most amazing singer ever, and you are going to slay in the talent show today."

"Exactly." Lucy nodded. "And then on Saturday, we can properly celebrate your success."

"Saturday?" Midnight said, worried that something else had slipped through her normally organized schedule.

"Don't worry. You haven't forgotten anything," Lucy teased. "We were going to tell you yesterday but you didn't show. Anyway, we're all going to the movies. That is, unless you have something else planned." This last part was accompanied by a telling look, no doubt as a reminder that Midnight had been less than reliable lately.

"Absolutely not. I'd love to go to the movies." She gave a vigorous nod of her head. Tabitha might pretend to be okay with being dumped by Sav, but Midnight had no intention of letting that happen to her.

"Good. Now, we want to get ready for the show," Sav said. "Will you come with us?"

"Um, I need to go to my locker. I'll meet you there," Midnight said, her grip tightening on the backpack. She wasn't sure of the school policy on carrying around deadly energy that could corrupt everything it touched, but she had a feeling it was probably frowned upon. She waited until her friends linked arms and headed in the other direction before letting out her breath.

"Thank goodness they've gone." Tabitha suddenly appeared, her normal mocking expression replaced by one of boredom. "Those girls sure can talk."

Midnight blinked. "Were you eavesdropping?" And why did everyone keep visiting her at her locker? Was there a sign above her head that said, Something Dangerous Is Hidden Here?

"Yeah. Because nothing says fun to me like hearing Savannah Hanson and Lucy Gibson spout out their little gems of wisdom," Tabitha deadpanned. She reached into her bag and pulled out a small vial of sludgy, red liquid. "Don't worry. I was just waiting until they left so I can ask you about this."

Midnight stared at the thick, red substance in the bottle. "Please tell me that's not blood."

"Of course it's not blood. It's chili sauce. Your mom posted the recipe on her blog and my mom tried it out. Unfortunately, something got lost in translation because it smells stronger than paint stripper."

"Wow, okay." Midnight's eyes watered as the overwhelming smell of red chilies hit her nose. "That definitely doesn't smell good."

"Right?" Tabitha gave a vigorous nod before carefully studying Midnight's face. "So I was hoping your mom could give my mom some tips before she poisons us. I love the cemetery, but I don't want to be buried there quite yet."

Midnight reluctantly took the vial. "I guess so."

"Thanks," Tabitha said, then pressed her lips together

in a thoughtful expression. "By the way, are you okay?"

"You mean apart from agreeing to ask my mom to do a forensic examination on chili sauce?" Midnight double-checked. "Yes, I'm fine. Why wouldn't I be?"

"Because you look like you haven't slept in a week. Plus, the way you were hugging your backpack when you were talking to Sav and Lucy was a dead giveaway."

"So you were spying?" Midnight widened her eyes, but Tabitha just gave an unrepentant shrug.

"I got bored. Anyway, here's a tip. If you don't want to look like you're hiding something, you need to lose the death grip."

"W-who said I was trying to hide something?" Midnight said in alarm.

Once again, Tabitha just shrugged. "Hey. It doesn't bother me either way. I'm just offering up some advice if you don't want your friends to suspect something. Anyway, we'd better get going if we don't want to be late for the talent show."

"Right." Midnight thrust the blood-like chili sauce into her locker next to the brass box containing enough spectral energy to contaminate an entire building. Then she followed Tabitha across to the school auditorium, so she could support Sav the way a good friend would. The last week had been crazy, but she was determined that from now on there would only be smooth sailing.

Chapter Seventeen

On Saturday, Midnight got ready to go to the movies
with Sav and Lucy. They were no longer angry with her.
The fact that Sav had won first place in the talent show
had probably helped. Still, all Midnight cared about was
that things were back to normal.

She reached for her good jeans and tried to decide
which sweater to wear. Lucy had liked them teamed up
with the purple one, but Sav had preferred the oversized,
white one with a cat face in the middle. Then she remembered that Lucy had eventually agreed that the white one
was cute. Cat it was.

Just as it was time to leave, the familiar ghost icon appeared on her phone's screen along with an address that was thirty minutes away. No. There was no way she'd be able to get there and back before the movie started. For the first time since she'd started her job, Midnight was seriously tempted to just ignore it. After all, it was just for one morning, and as soon as the movie was over, she'd be able to go to the address. But even as she thought it, she knew it wasn't an option. All she had to do was remember the hideous black veil of energy that had attached itself to Miss Appleby at the tire factory.

She swallowed hard as she reluctantly brought up Sav's number and made the call. There was no answer, and she was forced to leave a long, apologetic message. Then she grabbed her spectral transformer and her new black coat and headed downstairs.

The job was straightforward, but that was no consolation as Midnight climbed out of the taxi ninety minutes later and walked up to Miss Appleby's front door. Her friends were no doubt having a great time at the movies, while she'd been trying to get spectral energy out of a mailbox.

Not exactly the kind of weekend fun she'd been planning.

She knocked on the door, but after several sharp raps, there was still no answer. As she produced the key she'd been given the week before, she tried not to feel jealous that even Miss Appleby was probably having more fun.

"Hello?" She pushed open the front door, but there was no reply.

It was strangely silent without Miss Appleby's warm presence. Midnight made her way to the secret room, so she could separate the spectral energy from the glass plate.

Once it was finished, Midnight carried it outside. The dry grass crunched under her sneakers as she walked to the giant neutralizing tank. She didn't understand exactly how it worked, especially since as far as she could figure, it was never emptied. Then again, it wasn't like she understood how space travel worked either, so she pushed it from her mind.

She attached the glass bottle to the small tap at the bottom, so it could be sucked inside. Once the valve on the chamber closed, she removed the bottle and was just about to go home when the all-too-familiar sound of swarming bees rang out in her ear.

Midnight thrust her glasses over her nose in time to see a faint slither of pink fog dancing around one of the upstairs windows—the same fog that she'd seen at the cemetery. Her skin prickled as the fog drifted upward, like a feather. It disappeared through the window and materialized on the other side. Miss Appleby had assured her it was harmless, but as it continued to dance on the inside of the windowpane, Midnight wasn't so sure.

Whatever it was, it hadn't gone in there by accident.

She ran into the house, but it wasn't until her foot was on the first stair that she remembered that the second floor was out of bounds. Indecision gnawed at her. Of course she wanted to respect Miss Appleby's rules, but she couldn't just ignore what she'd seen. Surely pink fog trumped some damaged floorboards.

She took a deep breath and climbed the stairs.

Unlike the modern furniture downstairs, the hallway was filled with heavy antiques that seemed to close in on her as she passed by. There was no sign of any re-pair work, and by the time she reached the end of the hallway, her pulse was racing.

The room was sparse, with only a narrow twin bed and a wooden dresser. On the wall was a large oil painting of three people. She recognized George Irongate immediately from his distinctive handlebar mustache and small wire glasses. Next to him was his daughter, Elizabeth, who she recognized from the portraits in the study. There was also another woman who looked like a younger version of Miss Appleby, with the same aquiline nose and warm smile. Midnight paused and studied it.

It definitely wasn't his wife, Mary. However, judging by the resemblance to Miss Appleby, she could only guess that it was George's sister. Had he even had a sister?

She held up her phone and took a picture of the painting. Just then, the pink fog reappeared. Her hand dropped back to her side and she waited for the sickening numbness to overtake her like it always did when she was near spectral energy. Instead, a sleepy kind of warmth filled her. The fog wrapped itself around the portrait, then snaked its way over to the bed and disappeared underneath it. She frowned. Did it want her to follow?

Everything Miss Appleby had told her and all the

things that she'd read in the diaries screamed at her to run away, but somehow Midnight found herself lifting back the heavy comforter. There was no sign of the fog, but in its place was an old hatbox. The linen cover was faded and the latches rusted, and as she dragged it out, she was hit with a wave of dust.

Midnight sneezed as she pushed back the lid. Inside was a leather-bound diary similar to the ones in George's study downstairs. Next to the diary was a wooden box. The honey-colored timber was dull with age, and the brass hinges were green and tarnished. Inside was a tangle of wires and buttons along with a long brass nozzle poking out one side like a fire hose. It had to be another one of George Irongate's inventions.

She ran her finger along the smooth-grained wood and was just about to look through the diary when an engine rumbled to a halt outside the house, plunging her back into reality.

Midnight jumped back as guilt roiled inside her.

What was she doing, invading Miss Appleby's personal space?

Her cheeks heated as she quickly put everything away

and raced to the window. On the street below, she could see a taxi driver lifting shopping bags out of his trunk. Then he made his way around to the passenger side to help Miss Appleby.

Midnight raced downstairs and let herself into George Irongate's study. She tidied up the chemicals she'd been using earlier, her temples pounding with shame. What would Miss Appleby have thought if she'd caught Midnight rummaging through something that didn't belong to her?

What would her mom think? The idea caused her palms to prickle. She picked up a nearby spectral transformer and dismantled the flash, so she could clean it. The soothing action helped, and by the time Miss Appleby unlocked the front door, she was reasonably composed.

"Oh, dear. Please don't tell me that the alarm went off when I was out shopping?" Miss Appleby said as she walked into the room, her large brown eyes—so similar to her distant relative in the painting upstairs—filled with concern. "I'm so sorry. I foolishly thought that it would be safe to go."

"It's fine." Midnight went to escort the injured woman into the living room, but Miss Appleby shook her off with a small smile.

"No need. The doctor said the more I use it, the better it will be."

"Really? I thought it was going to be another couple of months."

"So did they, but I guess I'm just a fast healer." Miss Appleby gave a dismissive shrug. "So, tell me what happened."

"The spectral energy was in a mailbox on the other side of town." Midnight dropped into the spare chair. "But don't worry. It's all safely in the tank. Unfortunately, the taxi fare was out of this world. I'm really sorry about that."

"Please, child. You should know better than to apologize when you're the one who's doing me a favor," Miss Appleby scolded. "Now, where did I put my knitting?"

"I think it's still in the hallway." Midnight jumped to her feet. The knitting bag was sitting on a long white side table, and as Midnight picked it up, some of the amber yarn brushed her skin. She winced in pain as a cold slither twisted up her arm. Her throat tightened as a sense of darkness ran through her. *This is the second time it's happened.*

Then she saw that it had been sitting right next to one of the brass trinket boxes used to store the glass plates of spectral energy. She gave her arm a shake to try and get rid of the residual feeling and made a mental note to start wearing gloves in the future.

"Is everything okay?" Miss Appleby asked as Midnight walked back into the room.

"Fine." Midnight passed the knitting bag over and gave her arm another rub. "I forgot to put away one of the brass boxes and it gave me a zap."

"Oh." Miss Appleby sighed as she extracted her needles. "Definitely one of the downsides to this business. Now, are you going to confess what happened?"

"Confess?" Midnight's brow beaded with sweat. What if Miss Appleby had seen her in the window? "What do you mean?"

"I mean that you had plans to go see a movie with your friends, and I'm guessing that when the ghost app went off, you had to cancel. You can tell me that you're disappointed. It's only natural."

"Oh, yes," Midnight said, relieved. "The movies. It was bad timing, that's for sure."

"I hope they'll forgive you." Miss Appleby resumed her knitting. "Oh, and before I forget, I bought myself a cell phone. I decided it was time I joined the twenty-first century. The nice man set everything up for me except the ghost app. Would you mind showing me how it works?"

"Of course not," Midnight said. She spent the next ten minutes showing Miss Appleby the ghost app. "There. That should do it. Oh, but if you get a survey for the app, then don't reply to it or they'll just keep sending them. So far I've had about fifteen of them."

"Okay, I won't answer any surveys. And thank you. I'm still amazed that something so simple will be able to give me so much more freedom," said Miss Appleby.

Midnight was happy she could help Miss Appleby this much. She just hoped it didn't ruin her *own* social life.

CHAPTER EIGHTEEN

Midnight groaned as her alarm went off the following morning. She'd slept badly and her dreams had been peppered with numerous scenarios, all involving Sav and Lucy confronting her about missing the movie yesterday. Sometimes their only comments were about how her jacket didn't match her sneakers. But in most of the versions, they'd refused to ever speak to her again.

Each time Midnight had woken up, she'd tried to convince herself that it wouldn't be that bad, only to remember what had happened with the Logan saga. If she'd almost lost their friendship over that, then she hated to think what would happen because she stood them up. In the end, she'd gotten out of bed to start working on a preemptive strike.

As she stared at the flow chart in front of her, there was really only one conclusion, one common element which, if removed, would solve her problems and put an end to the nightmares.

She had to stop working for Miss Appleby.

What was the point of earning money to go on the ski trip of a lifetime if the people you wanted to go with thought you were a terrible friend?

Miss Appleby might be able to cope with not having any friends, but Midnight wasn't sure she could. She'd had to deal with that in Texas, and now she never wanted to be friendless again. Besides, Miss Appleby's ankle was almost healed, so it wasn't like she'd be left in the lurch.

Midnight got to her feet and walked to the kitchen. As usual, it was a chaotic mess. The counters were covered in freshly cut flowers and vegetables from the garden, and there was a pot of something boiling on the stove. Her mom was over by the sink chopping up onions, and Tabitha sat on a wooden stool, regaling her with something that had happened during history class on Friday.

Wait. *What?*

Midnight rubbed her eyes. Normally she only needed her glasses to see things at a distance, but that couldn't be right.

"Oh, hey, Midnight." Tabitha looked up, her painted black lips almost smiling.

Okay, so it was definitely Tabitha.

"Um, hey," Midnight said, resisting the urge to pinch herself. "Did I forget that we were meeting?"

"Relax. Your precious spreadsheet's safe," Tabitha assured her. "Your mom called about the chili sauce and said she had a few spare bottles. Apparently, the secret's balsamic vinegar."

"O-kay." Midnight blinked as she noticed the three bottles of sauce that were sitting next to Tabitha's backpack on the counter. It was turning into quite a surreal morning.

"It's an easy mistake to make," Midnight's mom explained. "And actually, before you go, I'll pick some lemons. My tree's bursting and your mom mentioned that she liked my lemon meringue pie recipe."

"Wow, she's so nice," Tabitha said as they both watched Midnight's mom make her way toward the lemon tree in the corner of the backyard.

"I guess." Midnight shrugged, used to the way her mom helped anyone who crossed her path. It was part of the reason why they'd never had any money until they'd inherited the house in Berry. It was also how she'd met Phil; they'd both stopped to help an elderly man who'd tripped at the grocery store.

"And sorry to turn up on your doorstep like this," Tabitha said. "Trust me, I'd much rather still be asleep, but my mom was in the middle of a soufflé crisis and she gave me an ultimatum: collect the chili sauce or go for a tennis lesson."

"Tough call." Midnight's lips twitched into a smile at Tabitha's pained face.

"Right." Tabitha gave a vigorous nod of her head just as Midnight's mom walked back in with an old wicker basket full of lemons. And after several last-minute instructions for Tabitha to pass on to her mom, she finally left.

"You never told me how lovely Tabitha was," Midnight's mom said. "You should have her over more often."

"Sure," Midnight said, wondering how Tabitha would cope with being called "lovely." Then she glanced at her phone and realized the time. "I need to go out this morning."

"Oh." Her mom, who had just gone over to stir the contents of the pot, looked up with interest. "Are you seeing Sav and Lucy?"

"As if." Taylor suddenly appeared in the doorway, her phone glued to her hand. Sometimes Midnight wondered if Taylor's neck would become permanently fused at a twenty-degree angle.

Midnight stiffened. "Why would you say that?" Had her sister heard something from Lucy's sister? Or, worse, had Midnight spoken out loud during her nightmares last night?

"Because I have eyes in my head." Taylor gave her a quick up-and-down glance. "You're wearing your oldest jeans and that black jacket looks like it belonged to someone in a vampire army—on the losing side.

When you go out with your friends, you have a vanilla cookie look."

"That's ridiculous." Midnight folded her arms, not sure whether to be relieved or offended.

"So you are going to meet Sav and Lucy?" Taylor raised an eyebrow.

Midnight gritted her teeth. "As it happens, I'm going to see Miss Appleby. Actually." Midnight coughed and turned back to her mom. "I've decided not to keep working for her."

"What?" Her mom stopped stirring the pot. Even Taylor looked up with interest. "I thought her ankle wasn't going to be fully healed for another two months."

"I know, but I've been finding it hard to manage everything, and her ankle's much better now."

Phil appeared at the back door, clutching at the wooden Viking shield he was making for her mom. Never had she been so happy to see him, and as her mom was busy exclaiming over the shield, Midnight took the opportunity to slip away.

The cool weather nipped at her skin, and Midnight thrust her hands deep in her pockets. As she walked, she tried to reassure herself that Miss Appleby would be okay with her decision. After all, she'd never once suggested that Midnight make it her life calling. Miss Appleby, out of everyone, would understand.

Midnight was so busy debating how to start the conversation that it wasn't until she reached the foot of Miss Appleby's porch that she saw the flicker of jagged, white light flash out from the side gate. She automatically thrust her glasses on, and the flashes were replaced by a cloud of something dark and repellent. A putrid smell hit her nose.

Whatever this was, it made spectral energy seem like a rainbow. She muffled a scream as waves of pain slammed into her body. Her limbs stiffened as her brain fogged with confusion. From where she was standing, she could see that the sickly cloud was hovering over the large lead-lined tank in Miss Appleby's backyard.

Was Miss Appleby inside her house? Or was she out in the backyard, already trying to deal with whatever this was? In the end, Midnight decided that the best thing to do was go straight through the yard.

She hurried to the side gate. To open it, she had to

stand on her toes and reach over for the lock, and, as she did so, she caught sight of Miss Appleby. Relief filled her. Whatever it was, Miss Appleby was already fighting it.

Midnight watched her crouch down in front of the tank and pull something out from the small tap.

It was yarn.

Miss Appleby was pulling yarn out of the tank?

Midnight's brow gathered. It didn't make sense. The dark cloud above the tank contracted, like it was in pain, but Miss Appleby didn't flinch. She just continued to wind the yarn into a large ball.

A thousand questions flooded Midnight's mind, but before she could try and answer them, she realized something else. *The yarn is the same pale pink color as the fog I have seen over the last few weeks.*

There had to be an answer, some kind of logical explanation. If only she knew what it was. She strained her neck as Miss Appleby finished winding the yarn and reached for her ever-present knitting needles and cast on.

Miss Appleby suddenly looked up from her work and Midnight's throat tightened. Gone was Miss Appleby's warm smile and smooth skin, and in their place were layers of lines running up and down gaunt skin framed by soft white tufts of hair. It was like the life had been sucked out of her and it was all Midnight could do not to scream out loud.

What was happening?

How was it happening?

But the only answer she got was from the spectral energy as it howled in fury and the wind swirled everywhere. Still Miss Appleby ignored it, the needles creating a sinister beat as each stitch was cast.

Midnight's feet were leaden. All she could do was watch as the lines on Miss Appleby's face softened and faded with each dip of the needle. Eventually, the spectral energy around the tank disappeared completely. Her employer gave a contented sigh as she put her knitting needles into the bag and made her way back into the house, her face once again familiar.

Midnight dropped back down and tried to catch her breath.

"Okay, what just happened?" a voice said and Midnight spun to see Tabitha standing farther along the fence line, her blue eyes clouded and her face drained of color.

CHAPTER NINETEEN

"W-what are you doing here?" Midnight's voice wasn't much louder than a squeak as she dragged Tabitha over to the far end of the fence, so they were hidden. Her heart was still hammering so loudly she almost thought it might explode from her chest.

"I forgot to give you this." Tabitha mutely fumbled in her skirt pocket and held up a USB drive, her eyes clouded with confusion. "S-so I went back to your house and your mom said you came here. I figured I was only a few minutes behind you. Then I saw you standing by the fence, so I thought I'd see what you were looking at…"

She trailed off, helplessly blinking.

"Right." Midnight forced herself to take the USB as she licked her lips. "You know you could've just emailed me the files."

"I'm starting to see the appeal of that," Tabitha agreed, her whole body shaking. "What just happened there?"

Midnight was silent as she tried to weigh the situation.

Truthfully, she had no idea herself. But even if she did, did she want Tabitha Wilson to know about it? Two things helped make her decision—the stubborn set of Tabitha's lips and the sudden noise from the back door, which made Midnight think that Miss Appleby might come back outside.

"Okay, but first we need to get out of here and we need to make sure that no one sees us."

"If by no one you mean Miss Appleby and her photoshopped face, then I have no problem with that."

They ran back down the street, not stopping for breath until they reached the safety of Midnight's room.

"Now." Tabitha collapsed onto the floor, her black skirts fanning out around her, making her look like a dark angel. "Please tell me what just happened."

Midnight was silent as she caught her breath.

If Tabitha decided to tell anyone else, then Midnight's experiences at her old school in Texas would be like a walk in the park compared to what would be in store for her. Then she let out her breath. A promise was a promise. Plus, she knew Tabitha wouldn't let it go until she had answers.

"Fine. But you have to swear not to tell anyone."

"Do I look like a gossip?" Tabitha raised an eyebrow.

Midnight let out a sigh as she sat down on the floor and crossed her legs. "Okay, besides, I guess it's only fair. After all, you were there at the beginning."

"The beginning?" Tabitha blinked. "What are you talking about?"

"Outside the school dance. I was dressed as a mouse and you were dressed—well, actually, you were just dressed as yourself. Anyway, that's when it all started…"

Half an hour later, Tabitha sighed. "So I was right. She is a witch."

Midnight winced. For someone who prided herself on planning everything from her homework to how long it would take her to eat a packet of M&M'S, she was doing a woefully bad job of explaining what it was exactly that Miss Appleby did. In her defense, it wasn't a conversation that she'd ever planned on having.

She also didn't know whether to be pleased or a little freaked out at just how well Tabitha had accepted the whole situation—a lot better than Midnight had handled it.

"I'm not even sure what she is." Midnight drew her knees up to her chin and let out a helpless sigh. She was numb from what she'd seen. "Which means I'm not sure what I am. What if everything she told me was a lie?"

"It can't all be a lie." Tabitha was examining the spectral transformer that Midnight had shown her. "You can definitely see this spectral energy stuff. And this camera is what helps you capture it? Which for the record is blowing my mind. I mean where are the stun guns and the ghost-busting backpacks?"

"Really? That's your question?"

"Sorry. I'm focused again. But she also gave you all of George Irongate's diaries to read, so she can't have made it all up." Tabitha continued to study the spectral transformer, her lips pushed together. Miss Appleby would freak if she knew that Midnight had shown it to anyone. Then again, it was Miss Appleby's fault in the first place that Midnight was even having the conversation with Tabitha.

"Well, yeah. Unfortunately, those things are true."

"Unfortunate? Are you kidding me?" Tabitha leaned forward. "I'm so jealous. It must feel so amazing to be able to see what no one else can."

"I'm not sure that's how I'd describe it. Most of the time I try not to think about it—or the fact that I'm different."

"You should be proud," Tabitha said with a flourish.

Midnight almost conjured up a smile as she tried to imagine how Tabitha would dress if she were the one who'd been born on Halloween. There would probably be a costume involved. However, the smile didn't last for long, as the images of Miss Appleby once again forced their way into her mind.

"Truthfully, right now I just want to figure out what happened," she said. "By the way, what exactly did you see when we were there?"

"Definitely no demonic black clouds or wind."

Tabitha let out a wistful sigh, obviously still annoyed at what she considered Midnight's good fortune. "But I saw her. One minute her face was so old that it looked like she might crumble, and then the next minute, it wasn't. If it's not witchcraft, what is it?"

"Your guess is as good as mine," Midnight said. She didn't really know anything about spectral energy other than what Miss Appleby had told her. Instead, she'd been happy to trust her, take what she said at face value—all because she was so desperate to earn enough money to go skiing. "If only I'd done more research. Asked a few more questions."

"You said that you read all of the diaries. Plus it wasn't like you made up the spectral energy. From what you've told me, it was there, right in front of your eyes the whole time. You had questions and she gave you answers."

"But what if they were the wrong answers?" Midnight shuddered. "I wish I knew what she was really doing."

"What are your thoughts on going back there and asking for an explanation?" Tabitha asked, a hopeful gleam in her eyes, but Midnight shook her head. To see Miss Appleby calmly standing there as the spectral energy swirled and raged around her, and then for her face to transform like that...There was no way Midnight could confront her.

"I can't. Even the idea of being near her is creeping me out."

"So we need to do this the old fashioned way." Tabitha didn't seem too upset as she cracked her knuckles. "Do you still have the diaries?"

Midnight shook her head. "No, I returned them all, and there was no mention of anything like what we just saw."

"Then I guess we'll have to rely on the good old Internet to find out everything we can about Natasha Appleby, George Irongate, and spectral energy."

"We?" Midnight folded her arms. It was one thing to tell Tabitha the truth, but it was another thing to drag her into whatever it was that was going on. "You really don't need to help."

"Don't need to help?" Tabitha looked at Midnight like she was crazy. "Hello, have you met me? You're combining research and spooky, strange behavior—my two favorite things. Besides, Mrs. Crown gave me the password to the school's genealogy software, so I can access it from here."

"The library has genealogy software?" Midnight raised an eyebrow.

"Yeah, though she doesn't tell many people. I think she has sharing issues." Tabitha grinned as she got to her feet. "Now, come on."

"Okay. Thanks." Midnight gave her a grateful smile as they opened up her laptop, and just like with their project, they quickly found themselves settling into a research routine. But after an hour, they hadn't found anything. Midnight was just about to suggest that they take a break when Tabitha frowned.

"Okay, this is weird. I'm looking at the Irongate family tree, but I can't see how Natasha Appleby can be part of that family."

"What do you mean?" Midnight leaned closer.

"George Irongate only had one brother, William, and according to this, he never married. Mary was an only child, and we know that Elizabeth died when she was twelve," Tabitha said before she wrinkled her nose. "Okay, wait. I might have something. Though it's weird."

"Weird? How's it weird?" Midnight said, trying to figure out what Tabitha's threshold for weird was considering everything they'd just seen.

"I've found details of George's second marriage."

"He was married twice?" Midnight's jaw dropped open. His diaries were written before his first marriage. Midnight hadn't realized he'd remarried after Mary died.

"Natasha Wright, born 1863. Daughter of Patricia Wright (née Appleby) and Phillip Wright," Tabitha read from the screen. "George died after just one year of marriage, and there were no children. But the really weird thing is that there's no death certificate for Natasha Irongate."

"Have you tried Natasha Appleby or Natasha Wright?"

"Yup, but still nothing. According to this, she's still alive."

"That doesn't make any sense." Midnight rubbed her forehead, willing the parts of the puzzle to fall into place. Then she froze. The painting in the upstairs bedroom. She'd assumed the woman with George and Elizabeth had been George's sister.

Except he didn't have a sister.

Yet the woman had an uncanny resemblance to Miss Appleby.

What if it wasn't just a resemblance?

Her throat tightened as she remembered the photograph in the locket she'd found. It had looked so much like Miss Appleby.

The air crackled with tension as Tabitha seemed to understand Midnight's conclusion. The pair of them were both silent, needing time to digest the possibility.

"But how can it be true?" Tabitha finally said, her voice a small croak. "I'm not a brainiac like Logan, but even I know that if your Miss Appleby is the same person, then it would make her over one hundred and fifty years old. But I've seen her at the cemetery and she doesn't look a day over fifty."

"Except today." Midnight's temples pounded as Miss Appleby's sunken, skeletal face flashed into her mind— and how life had only returned to it once she started knitting.

"Except today," Tabitha agreed, her whole body shaking. "Today she definitely looked that old. But there's something else that I can't quite put my finger on."

"What? Like the fact that she forgot to mention she was over one hundred and fifty-something years old and that the man who she said was her great-great-great-grandfather was really her husband?" Midnight wrapped her arms around her chest and tried to push down the rising nausea. But it was difficult.

Because if Miss Appleby had lied about her age and her relationship to George Irongate, then what else had she lied about?

"No. Yes. Grrrr, I don't know. There just seems to be a connection." Tabitha scrunched her face as she punched a pink throw pillow in distaste before reluctantly putting it down. "Sorry, natural reaction to that color. It's just so…pink! Of course, that's it!"

"A pink throw pillow is the answer?"

"No, idiot. Not the throw pillow. The color. The pink fog." Tabitha's entire face was animated as she jumped to her feet and began to march around the room. "Think about it. You only saw that strange, misty fog twice—once at the mausoleum and the second time was—"

"In the upstairs room of her house." Midnight widened her eyes as she realized what Tabitha was getting at.

"You think the pink fog wanted me to look under the bed and find the diary and weird invention?"

"That's exactly what I think. Which means we need to get them. Mrs. Crown always says that old letters and journals can give you the most valuable clues on where to look next. This is perfect." Tabitha's eyes lit up before she seemed to suddenly remember the situation. "Not that I'm condoning what we've just discovered of course."

"Of course not." Midnight momentarily smiled before shaking her head. "Unfortunately, we have no way of getting the diary, so it won't be much help."

"But what if it tells us something important?" Tabitha was now looking a bit like Taylor when she was trying to convince their mom to let her wear makeup. "And if you're worried about seeing her again, don't be. We could just wait until she goes out and then get it. After all, you still have a key, so it's not like we'll be breaking in. Well, not exactly."

"But that's the thing. She doesn't ever go out except when the flying arm electroscope goes off."

"That's it!" Tabitha exclaimed as she toyed with the long chain around her neck. Then she grinned. "Okay, here's the plan. You need to send Miss Appleby a text message to tell her you're feeling sick and that if the ghost app goes off, you won't be able to attend to it. Then, we go straight to her house, so we can see what's in that diary. Unless you have a better idea."

"How about inventing a time machine so we can go back and find the truth?"

"A better idea that's actually feasible," Tabitha amended, and Midnight shivered. Going anywhere near Miss Appleby's house again was the last thing she wanted to do. By a long shot. But Tabitha was right—this was their best chance. She reluctantly reached for her phone and sent Miss Appleby a text explaining just why she wasn't going to be available for the next couple of days. It took ten minutes for Miss Appleby to reply with an old-fashioned, well-punctuated message saying her ankle was much better and that she'd be able to cover any call-outs before wishing Midnight a speedy recovery.

Midnight put down her phone and swallowed her nausea. Now they just had to wait.

CHAPTER TWENTY

"I still think that my time-machine plan could've worked," Midnight said on Monday afternoon as she and Tabitha huddled behind a tree across the road from Miss Appleby's house. The ghost app had gone off fifteen minutes ago, and even though they'd both seen the old lady being driven off in a taxi, Midnight's stomach was churning. Perhaps she hadn't been lying when she'd told Miss Appleby she was sick—it would explain her shallow breathing and the pounding sensation in her chest.

"Midnight, if you really want to back out, there's still time," Tabitha said, some of her earlier bravado gone as the reality appeared to be sinking in. "We could find another way."

If only. Unfortunately, the pair of them had spent the rest of yesterday afternoon and most of the evening trying to figure out an alternative, and they'd come up blank. Midnight had even considered just pretending that none of it had ever happened. But after a sleepless night of tossing and turning with visions of Miss Appleby's sunken face and soulless eyes, she knew that denial wasn't an option.

"I'm sure," she said with more confidence than she felt.

"Then let's get going." Tabitha stepped out from behind the tree and began to cross the road.

"Wait? What? Tabitha, you can't come in." Midnight gave a firm shake of her head, causing her straight, brown hair to fly out in all directions. It was one thing for Tabitha to help her with some research, but it was another thing entirely to drag her into Miss Appleby's house and potential danger. Not to mention that Tabitha might not even be able to see what that danger was.

"Do you think I'm going to let you go in there alone?"

Tabitha demanded as she knitted her eyebrows together in a manner that Midnight was starting to become familiar with.

"Yes I do. Look, I got myself into this mess and—"

"And no offense, but there's no way you can get yourself out of it on your own," Tabitha retorted bluntly before softening her features. "I know you're only trying to be kind. But I want to help, and let's face it, you could use it."

"I don't understand why you'd want to." Midnight wrinkled her nose. "We don't know what Miss Appleby's capable of."

"You're right. But what I do know is that for the last three years of my life, not one person apart from my parents and Mrs. Crown has given me the time of day. You're the first one who hasn't thought I was a freak, Midnight," Tabitha said in an abrupt voice before rubbing her eyes as if to get rid of some dirt.

"That's not entirely true. The cemetery thing's definitely a bit freaky," Midnight said gruffly to disguise how touched she was. She of all people knew how good it felt to find friends. She looked up and gave Tabitha a grateful smile. "But thank you. I appreciate your help."

"Well, you should, because I'm awesome." Tabitha seemed to have recovered from whatever was in her eye. Midnight quickly followed. As they climbed the stairs to Miss Appleby's porch, she put her glasses on. After yesterday, she didn't want to take any chances.

"Hello?" Midnight called out as she slotted the key in and pushed open the door. Sweat beaded on her forehead as they both stepped inside.

"It looks so normal." Tabitha seemed disappointed as she took in the modern, bright decor.

"Unfortunately, it's not." Midnight closed the door and walked to the stairs. Their footsteps echoed as they reached the second-floor bedroom and Midnight was hit with an oppressive sensation. Even Tabitha lost some of her excitement as they stared up at the portrait of George, Elizabeth...and, undoubtedly, Miss Appleby.

"It's really her," Tabitha said, her voice little above a whisper. "She's been alive all this time."

Chapter Twenty-One

"But how's she doing it? What's her secret?" Midnight looked at George Irongate, as if willing him to give them some answers. His painted eyes stared back at her, unblinking. Midnight shuddered and hurried over to the bed. There was no pink fog to guide her this time, but when she lowered herself to the floor, the hatbox was exactly where she'd left it. She carefully dragged it out and lifted the lid.

Tabitha sucked in her breath as Midnight picked up the diary. It was dated 1894, the year before George and Elizabeth both died. The leather cover was dry and cracked with age, and when Midnight opened it, the pages creaked in protest, but she ignored it. She carefully turned the pages, using her finger to help read the faded, familiar writing.

She stopped at an entry dated August 1894 when she saw the name. Natasha. "Listen to this."

> Never did I think to find happiness again after my dear wife, Mary, died giving birth to our daughter. But three months ago, I met Natasha. She also has the sight and has suffered terribly trying to understand just what it was she was witnessing. After discovering that I'd been researching this phenomenon, she begged to help with my mission. To have someone who understands this terrible blight is so exhilarating. I have asked her to be my wife. We wed next week and I'm thrilled that she'll be able to become the mother that my beloved daughter, Eliza, so desperately needs. I feel blessed.

Midnight frowned and flicked further through the diary. She stopped when she reached December 1894.

Natasha made an astonishing discovery when she accidentally spilled some of the spectral energy from the storage tank. It had a strange effect on her skin and made it appear like that of a much younger person. I believe that there's something about the process of trapping it in the glass slides of the spectral transformer and then holding it in the tank that caused this strange event.

"But I don't understand." Tabitha, who'd been intently listening, wrinkled her brow. "Everything you've told me about spectral energy made me think it was evil. George Irongate just said it himself, so how could it help her stay young?"

"I don't know." Midnight gave a helpless shake of her head as she continued to scan the pages.

January 1895: I'm concerned about Natasha. The results of the spectral energy do not last, and so she's started to hunt it day and night to keep the tank filled and continue her experiments. She'll not listen to my reservations about using such a dangerous substance. I took a photograph of her last week, and when I developed it, I noticed a dark aura, like nothing I'd ever seen before. I'm convinced that she needs to stop with her line of inquiry. For everyone's sakes.

"I guess we know how that one ends," Tabitha said.

"If only I'd known this right at the start." The bile rose in Midnight's throat. "Remember I told you about the locket I found at the dance? Well, the photograph in that was the same. It was surrounded in black."

"Suddenly I'm questioning my favorite color." Tabitha sighed. "What else does it say?"

"Nothing good. This is from March 1895."

I am a fool. A complete fool. The spectral energy that I've spent my life fighting is actually not the dangerous essence that I have always thought it to be. Rather, it is a thing of pure goodness.

Midnight paused, exchanging confused glances with Tabitha.

She continued reading:

Every small wisp is a soul trying to move from one plane to the next. The Black Stream that exists around Berry marks it out as a doorway to the Afterglow. Which means that every particle of spectral energy I've hunted has been the essence of someone who once lived. My dear wife, Mary. My parents. Everyone.

And there's worse. I've discovered that the danger lies in keeping it trapped on this earthly plane rather than letting it pass through to the other side. The longer it's trapped, the more dark energy builds up, and that's been responsible for the horrific crimes that people have been committing. What on earth have I done? I've also noticed that the black aura that I saw in the last photograph has amplified and follows Natasha around like a hideous shadow. It's because of the knitting. She's started binding together strands of spectral energy, forcing them to release the life essence within. I believe that essence transfers directly into the closest human it can find. Her.

"Hideous shadow?" Tabitha blinked. "Have you noticed it?"

Midnight shook her head. "No, never. Though I'd

have to be wearing my glasses and I only do that when there's already spectral energy around," she said before pausing, her throat tight. "The second time we went out, she was covered in spectral energy, but she told me it was because it had been building up for a long time."

"So, it could've been her hideous shadow?" Tabitha whispered.

Midnight rubbed her brow as more pieces of the puzzle fell together. "Her ankle. The doctors thought that it would take another two months to heal, but it's almost better."

"It all makes sense," Tabitha said before catching Midnight's horrified look. "I mean in a totally sick, twisted way. We need to look for what we can do to stop Miss Appleby. See if you can find anything else about this wooden box. Surely it's here for a reason."

Midnight forced the nausea back and continued to turn the pages until she found an entry that included a detailed diagram of the strange box.

May 1895: I've invented a way to reverse the damage I've caused. I believe that unlike the spectral transformer, which attracts the energy to the glass plate and traps it, this electro-pulse converter will do the opposite. It will send out an electrical charge to change the polarity of the trapped particles and let them cross to the Afterglow. With this, the dark energy that's been building up should dissolve. I've already tested the weapon once on the storage tank, but unfortunately it didn't work. However, I'm recalibrating some of the settings and will test it again this week. But for now I must go, because all is not well. My beloved Eliza is sick and Natasha's constantly arguing with me about the spectral energy. I will not let her succeed. I will right the terrible wrong that I have done.

"I don't understand. Did he finish making this thing work? If so, why didn't it stop her?"

"Because this was written two days before Elizabeth died and only five days before his own death." Midnight's voice trailed off and they sat in silence as the truth descended on them like a shroud.

Whatever had happened to George and Elizabeth had stopped him from releasing the spectral energy. It also meant that Miss Appleby had been trapping it since their deaths, way back in 1895. And the only thing that might have stopped her was the injury she received four weeks ago. Until Midnight had come along and helped her.

A lump formed in her throat, and it took all of her willpower not to burst into tears at what she had done. All of this for some stupid ski trip. What kind of person did that make her?

"Okay, so there's only one way to find out if this machine works. Let's go downstairs and try it on the tank," Tabitha said. "Then hopefully this thing will be over once and for all."

"First we have to figure out how to start it." Midnight forced back her guilt as she picked up the electro-pulse converter and compared it to George's detailed sketch. "The cameras were all mechanical, so they didn't require a power source, but if this uses electricity, there must be a way to turn it—oh no."

"What does *oh no* mean?" Tabitha leaned forward, concern written across her face.

"It means that there's something missing. Look." Midnight pointed to a sketch of a glass cylinder about the size of her fist. According to George Irongate's notes, it was meant to fit along the side of the electro-pulse converter.

"I was really hoping that you wouldn't say that." Tabitha picked up the hatbox and lifted away the delicate tissue paper, but apart from the overwhelming smell of camphor, it was empty. "Okay, we have to try not to panic."

"Try not to panic?" Midnight blinked. The blood pumped through her temples as the enormity of what it meant sank in. She knew what Miss Appleby was doing and she had no way to stop it. "How can I not panic? We've got a weapon with a missing part and no idea if it actually works. More to the point, we have no idea what to do if it doesn't work. If ever there were a time to panic, now is that time. I've messed up so bad. It's all my fault."

"That's ridiculous. The only thing you did wrong was to believe Miss Appleby when she explained to you what all the weird stuff was that you kept seeing and feeling. All you were doing was looking for an explanation."

"And I found the wrong one." Midnight's voice cracked.

"You're welcome to send me an invitation to your pity

party once this is all over, but right now we need to get to work. We need to find this glass thing, and the sooner we start looking, the better."

Midnight stayed silent, and she swallowed the tears that were threatening to overwhelm her. Tabitha was right. There would be time enough for that later on. She got to her feet and rolled up her sleeves.

"You're right. We still have about half an hour to search the house. But I think one of us should be the lookout. Because—"

"Running into an evil one-hundred-and-fifty-year-old woman who likes to kill people isn't a good idea?" Tabitha finished off, the color draining from her face. "I agree. Which means we need to be quick. This place gives me the creeps."

"That makes two of us." Midnight picked up the converter, lowered it into the large backpack she always carried, and then put the diary on top of it. The sooner they found the missing part, the better. The alternative didn't bear thinking about.

Chapter Twenty-Two

Normally when Midnight wanted to solve a problem, she'd do so in a logical way: with bullet points and color-coded flow charts. Unfortunately, as she stared at the electro-pulse converter on Tuesday morning, she knew that it was going to take more than organization to fix it—like a miracle, or at least another chance to search Miss Appleby's house, because they hadn't found anything.

Until the ghost app went off again, they wouldn't be able to go back. And if Miss Appleby realized that they'd taken the diary and the converter, they'd be in all kinds of trouble. Midnight let out a frustrated sigh just as her mom poked her head around her bedroom door.

"Just wanted to check that you're okay. You've been quiet the last few days."

Midnight quickly threw a sweater over George Irongate's invention. "I'm fine," she assured her mom, avoiding eye contact. After she'd returned from Miss Appleby's house, she'd spent the rest of the evening trying to figure out how the electro-pulse converter actually worked, but all she'd achieved was a headache. She got to her feet and went through the motion of stacking her books into her backpack.

"Well, I just wanted to say how proud I am. You've worked hard to pay for your ski trip, and you've helped Miss Appleby at the same time. Oh, and you've started wearing your glasses more."

Midnight's cheeks burned at the misguided compliment. If her mom knew the truth, she wouldn't be quite so proud. As for wearing her glasses, that was only because she was terrified of what else she might miss without them.

She dipped her head and fiddled with her pencil case, but before she could reply, her phone beeped. She quickly glanced at the screen, glad of an excuse to avoid her mom's gaze. It was Tabitha saying that Mrs. Crown was already at the library and had allowed Tabitha down into the basement stacks.

"I'd better go."

"Of course. But don't forget to at least grab a waffle on your way out. You can't save the world on an empty stomach."

Midnight's embarrassment increased as she quickly made her way to school, the gray sky exactly matching her mood.

The library doors were open, but Midnight didn't want to risk annoying Mrs. Crown again so she decided to wait outside. She shoved a hand into her pocket to retrieve George Irongate's diary when she heard a soft buzzing noise. She scanned the buildings around her. At first she couldn't see anything and she was just about to return to the diary when she noticed a tiny flicker of spectral energy dancing through the sky. With its pale, delicate tendrils, it reminded her of a snowflake. Midnight gasped as she saw a second one. It quivered in the air before darting upward and reappearing only feet from where she was standing.

Was it playing?

She held her breath as a third tiny spark of energy danced into her vision. How had she ever thought that spectral energy could be evil? That it could hurt anyone? It was clear that the energy only emitted darkness and pain when it was trapped and wanted to be free. This was its natural state. Without thinking, Midnight extended her arm to see if the energy would touch her.

"Midnight, there you are. We were starting to think you'd been abducted," Sav's voice rang out. She turned to where Lucy and Sav were standing, the delicate spectral energy forgotten. She'd sent them a few text messages yesterday, but there hadn't been any reply, which meant she had no idea how angry they were with her.

"I'm so sorry," Midnight wailed as she tried to recall if she was wearing her good jeans. A quick glance down told her she had. That was one thing in her favor. "You have no idea how bad I feel about it."

"And so you should. You missed the most amazing day ever," Lucy said, the angry lines around her mouth softening.

"Really?" Midnight said, relieved that she seemed to be off the hook. "What happened?"

"We met these two guys at the movies on Saturday and then we followed them to the park," Lucy explained.

Sav nodded before her eyes filled with annoyance. "But by the time we got there, they were just leaving and didn't even notice us. So now we've got no way of figuring out who they are. You have no idea how frustrating it is."

Midnight wanted to tell them that compared to what she was trying to solve, tracking down a pair of cute guys didn't even seem like a blip on the radar. Instead, she bit her lip as Tabitha came running toward her. Her black hair billowed out behind her and numerous silver chains clattered around her neck. She was clutching a folder in her hand and was still panting as she came to a halt.

"Sorry to interrupt. But I kind of need to speak to you," Tabitha said, her blue eyes so wide that Midnight thought they might be in danger of popping.

"Oh, you've got to be kidding me." Lucy folded her arms and turned to Midnight. "Tell your friend that we're having a private conversation."

"Like *really* need to speak to you," Tabitha elaborated, wriggling her eyebrows in some kind of code. She protectively hugged the folder to her chest.

"Actually," Midnight said to Lucy. "I think it's important."

"Important?" This time it was Sav who spoke, her lips curled in disgust. "You're doing a freaking local history project together. You know, Midnight, I think it's about time you sorted out your priorities. The thing that really gets me is Lucy wanted me to wash my hands of you after you betrayed me with Logan, but I didn't. I supported you."

"I didn't betray you with him," Midnight reminded her, once again hit by the irony that she could be accused of flirting with Logan when, in reality, she couldn't even string a sentence together in his presence. Then she remembered that she'd spoken to him twice since then, and while she still wasn't sure how she felt, she did know it wasn't indifference. She licked her lips. "I thought you didn't like him."

"So not the point, Midnight." Sav now had two small balls of color in her cheeks. "Lucy and I were the only ones who could see something special in you, who worked tirelessly to help you uncover your true potential, and all you've done is thrown it back in our faces. I'm just not convinced you want to be friends with us, let alone go skiing."

What? Midnight's stomach churned as Sav's words hung in the air like a knife. Even Tabitha sucked in her breath.

"Of course I do," she said. How could Sav even suggest otherwise? Everything Midnight had done had been for that very purpose. It was even the reason why she'd gone around to Miss Appleby's house to quit her job, because the ski trip with Sav and Lucy meant so much. She'd worn a mouse costume for them. She'd potentially helped an age-defying old woman do something that she shouldn't have been doing...

Her protest faded and was replaced by a dull throb in her brow.

"If you want to be our friend, then you need to prove it. And that means not being seen hanging out with a freak like Tabitha Wilson. I mean, look at what she's wearing," Lucy said, almost sounding like a parrot.

The air hummed with tension. This was it, her worst fears come to life.

Tabitha's face tightened at their ultimatum.

Midnight opened her mouth, but it was impossible to speak.

All Tabitha had ever done was try to help her. In fact, she'd hardly blinked when Midnight had told her about spectral energy. Yet Sav and Lucy wanted her to ignore Tabitha like she was no one.

Shame filled her. If fitting in meant being rude to people she liked, then perhaps she shouldn't keep trying to fit in.

"Well?" Lucy demanded in such a sharp voice that even Tabitha jumped.

Midnight stiffened her spine and dug her nails into the flesh of her arm to stop herself from being scared. "I'm sorry, but I really need to speak to Tabitha."

"You are so unbelievable," Sav hissed, her brilliant golden eyes narrow. "What makes it worse is that I put my reputation on the line. I thought that we could turn you into someone cool. But I was wrong. Your invitation to the ski trip is off the table, obviously. Come on, Lucy.

The smell of freak makes me want to puke."

Then, without another word, the two girls walked away, arms linked. Midnight blinked as they headed toward the quad, complaining bitterly as they went. So that answered her question about them being supportive and understanding.

"Are you okay?" Tabitha said in a soft voice.

"I guess," Midnight admitted. She tried to ignore how much her hands were shaking as the reality hit her. The thing that she'd feared the most had just happened. She'd tried to fit in and was found wanting. She was on the outside again. Except right now it seemed like the least of her problems.

"When I got friend-dumped, Sav poured a whole can of soda down my shirt, then said at least no one would notice it against the black fabric."

Midnight's jaw dropped. "That's horrible."

"Actually, it's immature and character revealing, and getting away from Savannah Hanson and her narcissistic drama was the best thing that ever happened to me," Tabitha corrected. She didn't look at all bothered by how she'd been treated.

"You never told me how you felt about her."

"Talking about other people behind their backs is more Sav's style than mine." Tabitha shrugged as she walked toward a nearby bench. Midnight followed her over. "Anyway, we have more important things to discuss. But you might want to sit down. It's pretty disturbing."

"I've watched spectral energy come out of a wheelbarrow, seen an old lady change her face with some knitting, and just been ditched by two of the most popular girls in school. I think I'm safe." Midnight gave her a bitter smile.

"Don't say I didn't warn you." Tabitha carefully opened up her research folder and brought out a piece of paper. "It's the death certificates for George Irongate and his daughter, Elizabeth."

Midnight sat down.

"How did you get these?" she asked, her voice not much more than a croak.

"Mrs. Crown. I think she's a hacker. Or a ninja. Or a ninja hacker. But here's the kicker: they both died of arsenic, which according to Mrs. Crown was the poison of choice in the nineteenth century. Do you know what this means?"

"Miss Appleby really did kill them." Midnight's hands shook as she studied the certificates. It seemed like the deeper they scratched, the worse everything became.

CHAPTER TWENTY-THREE

Taylor wandered into the kitchen on Friday afternoon looking smug in a new sweater. "Midnight, there's no point checking your phone every two seconds. They're not going to call."

"Who's not going to call?" Their mom looked up with interest, and Midnight froze. She'd actually been doing an Internet search to figure out what the missing part of the electro-pulse converter did. So far, her most promising lead was that it was some kind of battery or power source. She and Tabitha had been waiting all week for another chance to get into Miss Appleby's house, but they hadn't had one yet. All she knew was that she had to find a way to destroy Miss Appleby. That or go crazy. Because ever since they'd discovered the truth, it was all Midnight could think about—to try and figure out a way to fix the mess she'd made.

"Sav and Lucy," Taylor said. "Lucy's sister told me that Midnight got friend-dumped for being a loser."

Midnight longed to correct her annoying sister. *Actually, I got friend-dumped for spending too much time catching spectral energy for a one-hundred-and-fifty-something-year-old woman who turned out to be an evil, image-obsessed murderer.* Wisely, she kept her mouth shut.

"What?" Their mom put down the potato she'd been peeling, her face full of alarm. "Midnight, why didn't you mention this?"

"Because it's no big deal," Midnight said evenly. Her mom walked over to the table, which meant she wanted an explanation. Midnight put down her phone and sighed. "I'm fine. Really. Sav and Lucy don't like Tabitha, and they gave me an ultimatum. I didn't want to say anything because I didn't want you to worry."

"Worry's my middle name. Do you think that things will get better?"

Midnight thought of the pointed glares and whispered conversations that had been directed at her over the last couple of days. She'd seen Sav and Lucy in action before, though she never thought that she'd be on the receiving end. She also knew that as far as her friends were concerned, there was no going back.

"Maybe," she said vaguely, to stop her mom from worrying.

"It explains why you've been so distracted lately." Her mom reached and took her hand. "And why you didn't tell me about Miss Appleby."

"W-what do you mean?" Midnight's pulse quickened, and it took all of her willpower not to tighten her grip on her mom's hand. Did this mean that Miss Appleby had discovered the diary and the electro-pulse converter were missing?

"She called yesterday to ask if you were feeling better because she was worried that she hadn't heard from you. What's going on, Midnight? I thought you were going to quit that job. Why did you tell her you were sick?"

"Oh." Midnight's head began to swim. Why hadn't she made a spreadsheet to keep track of all of her deceptions? "I guess I was just feeling overwhelmed with everything. W-what did you tell her?"

"I told her that as soon as you were feeling better you'd stop by," her mom replied, pursing her lips.

"I will, and sorry I didn't tell her. I was just waiting until the thing with Sav and Lucy had blown over," she lied. Truthfully, she was waiting until she found the missing part of the electro-pulse converter before she gave Miss Appleby her front-door key back.

"It's okay," her mom relented, just as the ghost app rang out.

Midnight reached for it and studied the screen. It was for a location on the other side of town. Tabitha had also downloaded the app, so Midnight wasn't surprised when her friend sent a text message several seconds later suggesting they head over immediately. Her heart pounded as she got to her feet.

"Do you mind if I meet Tabitha for an hour or so?"

"I guess not." Her mom's lips twitched. "Don't forget to be back here before six because we're going out with

Phil to have dinner at the Country Kitchen. We're considering using it for the wedding venue, so we want to try it out first."

"Okay." Midnight gave an absent shrug, then grabbed her winter coat and quickly put it on. Normally she would've been happy at the news that they weren't going to use a Viking feast hall, but right now it didn't seem to matter.

"At least we know she wasn't lying about feeling sick," Taylor drawled. "Because she just agreed to go to dinner with Phil without rolling her eyes or moaning. I think it could be fatal."

"You're so hilarious, Taylor. Really, I just can't stop laughing," Midnight retorted. She said a quick goodbye to her mom, poked her tongue out at her sister, and hurried out the door.

Midnight met Tabitha two doors down from Miss Appleby's house. "I just saw her pull away in a taxi," Tabitha said. Then she frowned. "Are you okay? You look pale."

"Miss Appleby called my mom to see how I was feeling. We really have to find it soon."

"Agreed. Though I might have a lead. My dad was talking to the contractor about getting a fireplace, and the contractor started rambling on about how his old house had a hiding spot behind the chimney in the attic. Perhaps that's what George did to keep it safe? It has to be worth a shot."

"Definitely," Midnight agreed. She took a deep breath and opened the front door. Every time they stepped inside, the house was colder and more uninviting. Tabitha headed straight up to the attic, and Midnight went back to the room where they'd first discovered the diary. The plan was to continue searching through the numerous boxes stored under the bed.

As she pulled the first one, the old wooden floor creaked and dust rose softly up into the air, as if complaining about the disturbance. It reminded Midnight of the tiny slithers of spectral energy that she now saw wherever she went. The first box was filled with books so old that the covers crackled as they were touched. In the second one, she came across an envelope of photographs and was greeted by the smiling face of Elizabeth Irongate.

Midnight bit down on her lower lip as she tried to imagine what it must feel like to be poisoned. Tabitha had looked it up on the Internet, and some of the symptoms included vomiting, headaches, cramping, and convulsions until the body finally shut down altogether.

Had Elizabeth even known what was happening to her?

Had she been angry about it? Had she—

"I thought I told you not to come up here," Miss Appleby said. Midnight looked up to see the older woman standing there, her dark eyes cold and menacing.

CHAPTER TWENTY-FOUR

The walking stick was gone and her honey-colored hair was almost as golden as Sav's. Her skin was soft and dewy, like a cartoon character. She looked amazing.

Unfortunately, Midnight now knew that it wasn't a good thing.

She closed her eyes and swallowed. What was she supposed to do now? Run? Hide? Scream? Or all of the above? She opened her eyes again, but Miss Appleby was still standing there, eyes blazing.

"Y-you also told me that spectral energy was evil," Midnight said, amazed that the words came out louder than a whisper. "I saw you at the tank this past weekend, and I know what you're doing."

Miss Appleby's jaw tightened, a flicker of emotion crossing her face. Then she shrugged. "You're a reasonably smart girl, so I suppose it was only a matter of time."

Midnight's face heated. It was one thing to piece all the clues together, but it was another thing to listen to Miss Appleby confirm it.

Everything she'd said was a lie.

A lie that Midnight had believed.

"You have no idea how draining it is just to stay alive," Miss Appleby said, her voice cold. "Of course, the accident didn't help. Not only did I need extra energy to heal, but it made it almost impossible for me to get that energy. I was in quite a fix until you appeared on my doorstep, like a gift."

Midnight's head spun as the words sank in. There was no remorse.

"You won't get away with it," Midnight said. "I have the electro-pulse converter."

Miss Appleby burst out laughing. "Should I tell you a little secret? The reason I leave it here is because it's a reminder of what happens to those who don't listen to me. I begged George not to make it, but he ignored me."

"So you killed him just so that you could live longer?" Midnight's voice was thick with tension.

"Of course." Miss Appleby gave her a closed-lipped smile, as if killing her husband hadn't even been a decision. "It's not like I didn't warn him."

"And Elizabeth? Did you warn her?"

"Elizabeth was a complication." Miss Appleby almost looked wistful. "But don't expect me to regret what I've done, because I don't. And I should tell you that your little weapon won't work. I destroyed the part you're looking for. There's nothing you can do to stop me."

The glass piece has been destroyed?

Midnight's heart seized. Without the piece to run the weapon, the souls trapped in the tank were stuck there forever. She couldn't save them.

But she could still stop Miss Appleby.

Tabitha was up in the attic, and with any luck, she'd seen Miss Appleby arrive. Hopefully she'd called the police or managed to get herself to safety. Either way, Midnight needed to try and buy her friend some time. It was the least she could do.

"I still don't understand how it even works. How can knitting spectral energy make you younger?"

"Because when the strands of spectral energy are bound together, it expels the essence that once kept the souls bound to their physical bodies. That essence automatically transfers to the closest host it can find. Me."

Bile rose in her stomach. "That's horrible. You won't get away with this. I'll tell people what you're doing," Midnight said.

"Who are they going to believe, you or me?" Miss Appleby laughed.

"Well, I still won't let you trap any more souls. I won't let you steal their essence." Midnight gritted her teeth. "Even if I have to turn up every time the ghost app goes off, I'll make sure that you can't hurt any more spectral energy."

"Poor Midnight. You still don't understand the delicious irony. You see, up until four weeks ago, there was no way I could ever have left Berry. Without the flying arm electroscope, I couldn't have survived. But you changed all that with your app. You've opened up the world to me. There are at least fifty Black Streams in America alone, not to mention Europe and Asia."

Midnight let out an involuntary gasp. "You said Berry was the only one."

"I lied." Miss Appleby shrugged. "I'd planned to leave next month after I'd collected enough spectral energy to prepare me for the journey. But it looks like I might have to leave tomorrow."

"Why are you going tomorrow?" Midnight's temple pounded. If Miss Appleby left Berry, then no one would ever be able to stop her.

"Because I have to deal with you, and I'd prefer not to be around for the aftermath." Miss Appleby pulled out a knife, the blade glinting in the sun. "And if you think you can outrun me, you're wrong. You see, the more spectral energy I have, the stronger I become. And trust me when I tell you that I've had a lot of spectral energy."

Midnight's throat tightened. So that explained why she looked so youthful. She must have been knitting up a storm.

"If it's any consolation, I did really like you, Midnight. You reminded me of myself."

"Except I'd never kill anyone. And if I'd known what you were really doing with the spectral energy, I never would've helped." Midnight tried to edge away.

"That's true." Miss Appleby sighed, as if she was used to being disappointed. She took another step forward, the blade now dangerously close. "Oh, and don't expect your friend in the attic to help you. She's locked in, and after I've dealt with you, she'll be next."

"You can't." It was bad enough that she was in danger, but Tabitha didn't deserve any of this.

"Actually, I think you'll find that I can," Miss Appleby corrected, just as a tendril of pale pink fog swirled out from the portrait of Elizabeth Irongate. Midnight let out a small gasp, but Miss Appleby just stood there, oblivious.

She didn't have her glasses on, which meant she couldn't see it.

Midnight sucked in a sharp breath as more fog billowed out of the portrait and into the room, moving in a circle to create a small whirlwind. The bed shook and the curtains began to whip the air.

"What's going on?" Miss Appleby lifted her hand and

stared as the wind pried open her fingers one by one. The knife clattered to the floor, and Midnight ducked under Miss Appleby's flailing arms and raced out the door, stopping only to lock it behind her. At the top of the attic stairs, she could hear Tabitha yelling. Thankfully, the key was still in there and she quickly turned it.

"Oh my—" Tabitha started to say, but Midnight just grabbed her hand and dragged her down the stairs.

"Come on. We have to get out of here. Fast."

"Sounds like a plan to me," Tabitha panted as they raced across the landing. From the spare bedroom, Midnight could hear Miss Appleby cursing, but she still hadn't managed to break out. She urged Tabitha to go faster, but it wasn't until they were three blocks away that they came to a halt.

"I knew there was a reason that I didn't play any sports." Tabitha leaned over to catch her breath before she finally straightened up. "So, tell me what happened? Are you okay? How did you get away?"

"It was the pink fog." Midnight took a deep breath and hitched her backpack higher on her shoulder. "I think it's the ghost of Elizabeth Irongate. She came out of the painting and pushed the knife from Miss Appleby's hand. I think she's been trying to warn me this whole time."

Tabitha tugged at her black hair. "Two days ago that might have sounded ridiculous, but now it actually sounds feasible. I don't suppose she helped you find the missing piece while you were there?"

"I have some bad news. Miss Appleby destroyed the missing piece. That's the only reason why she kept the machine around, because she knew it didn't work." Midnight's bottom lip began to wobble as the reality of what had happened hit home.

"Do you think she might be lying?"

"Why would she lie about that when she was so happy to confess to everything else?" Midnight's throat tightened. "And that's not the worst of it."

"How can it get worse than almost being killed by a one-hundred-and-fifty-year-old woman?" Tabitha demanded. "And look, I know that being peppy isn't normally my thing, but we can't give up."

"I wish it were that easy. Unfortunately, thanks to the fact that I taught her how to use the ghost app, she can

CATHERINE HOLT

now leave Berry for the first time since 1895. And once she leaves, we'll have no chance of stopping her."

They'd failed. And it was all Midnight's fault.

223

Chapter Twenty-Five

As Midnight walked into the Country Kitchen with her mom, Phil, and Taylor that night, she knew she was in for a rough evening. The restaurant was cute enough—it had long chalkboard menus, mason jars crammed with lavender, and wide trestle tables made out of old barn doors. Even the food smelled nice. But she couldn't get the events at Miss Appleby's house out of her head. And then she saw that Sav and Lucy were there with Sav's fancy lawyer father and society mom.

None of this was helped by the fact that Midnight's mom was wearing a bright-purple, Mexican embroidered top with equally bright red jeans, and Phil had on his favorite Sons of a Gunnar T-shirt for the occasion. Midnight was pretty sure that even the blind woman at the far end of the restaurant turned to look at them with interest.

"You really must be the unluckiest girl around." Taylor snickered. "Still, at least you're not wearing a mouse costume."

"They're the least of my worries," Midnight sighed, following the waiter to their table.

Sav and Lucy pointedly ignored her.

"Are you okay?" Taylor narrowed her eyes.

"Fine. Great. On top of the world." Midnight bit her lip and willed herself not to cry. The worst thing about seeing Sav and Lucy was that it reminded her of just what a bad judge of character she was. After all, she'd been friends with two girls who'd been rude to Tabitha and Logan, not to mention half the other kids in their class. Yet Midnight hadn't even cared because she'd been too busy congratulating herself on being popular. As for Miss Appleby, Midnight had been even blinder.

She'd messed up so badly, and now there was no way to stop it.

Miss Appleby could go anywhere, and what was to prevent her from changing her name or the color of her hair? She would just fall off the radar and keep capturing innocent spectral energy, regardless of the consequences.

"Look." Taylor fell into step with her. "I shouldn't have given you a hard time. The truth is that those girls are toxic and you can do better than them."

"Thanks." Midnight blinked, half waiting for the other shoe to drop.

Instead, Taylor reached out and squeezed her hand. "Don't mention it." Her sister smiled and while it didn't stop Sav and Lucy from glaring, Midnight managed to walk past them without crying. Unfortunately, that proved to be the highlight of the evening, and by the time she crawled into bed, her head was pounding.

Her dreams were peppered with images of Elizabeth Irongate. Her face kept disappearing and being replaced with pale pink fog, begging Midnight to stop the woman who'd taken her life and that of her father. But instead of standing up and helping them, Midnight just laughed and held a car door open so that Miss Appleby could drive away. It was like assisting Darth Vader in getting the Father of the Year award.

By the time it was morning, Midnight was almost pleased to get up. She groggily put on her glasses and walked to the window. It had become her habit to stare at the tiny wisps of spectral energy floating around, waiting to pass across to the Afterglow where they would be safe.

Unless Miss Appleby got to them first.

Midnight took her glasses off and turned away, only to catch sight of the electro-pulse converter sitting useless on her desk. Suddenly the idea of having it in her room made her ill. What was the point of keeping it when it didn't work? And even if she could fix it, Miss Appleby would be gone by the end of the day.

She gathered it up and marched downstairs. The sooner it was gone, the better. But it wasn't until she walked into the kitchen that she realized Phil was there. He was wearing a gray tunic with embroidery around the neckline that was barely visible thanks to the heavy metal pendant hanging there. On his head was a fur-lined hat the size of a house. The table was covered with a sword, a leather belt, and some kind of thing that had a chain attached to it—just in case she thought her day couldn't get any worse.

"It's okay." Phil stood. "I'm just on my way out. We've got a big battle next week and we still need to work on our shield techniques."

"Um, that's nice," Midnight said, reminding herself that she'd promised to be polite. Besides, she wasn't actually annoyed at Phil; she was more annoyed with herself for failing the world. Big time.

"Now, that looks interesting," he said, noticing the electro-pulse converter. "Let me guess, late-nineteenth century? Locally made, judging by the Virginian pine timber, though I've never seen an electromagnetic battery modified like that before."

Midnight's jaw dropped. "Y-you know what this is?"

"Sure, they were used to deliver electric shocks to patients during the Victorian era. We have several of them in the museum." Color rose in his cheeks. "Okay, I didn't mean to say that."

"Say what?" Midnight blinked.

"About the museum," he said as he sat back down and let out a sigh. "If any of the Gunnars knew that I did a bit of work for the Berry American History Museum, I'd never hear the end of it. The museum claimed that Vikings weren't technically part of American history and refused to donate to help us build a longboat. Ever since, they've been feuding. But I like fixing things, so I've helped them maintain some of the equipment."

"Wait, you actually know how this thing works?" Midnight's pulse quickened. Was this some weird dream too? One where Phil was telling her that he wasn't just her mom's annoying fiancé who dressed like a Viking, but that he actually knew how to fix the converter?

"Pretty much." He gave her one of his goofy nods, but this time Midnight didn't mind it. "But there's something different about this. It's been modified, and of course, it's missing the main capacitor."

"Capacitor? What's that?"

"They're used to store energy in an electric field. My guess is that this one would've been made of glass."

"S-so if I wanted to get one of the capacitors, how would I go about that?" Midnight said, hardly daring to move.

"It would cost a fortune to buy an original, but if you just wanted to make the machine work, I'd be happy to rig you up one. It wouldn't look pretty, but it would do the job."

"You could really do that?" Tears prickled in the corners of her eyes. She might still have a chance.

"Sure," Phil said. "We could head over to the garage now if you like. I'm not due at the park for another hour. Tell you what, you go get ready, and I'll call your mom to let her know what we're doing."

"I—" Midnight paused, uncertain of how she could fully express her gratitude. In the end, she just gave him a shy smile. "Thank you."

"Don't be silly. It's my pleasure." Phil beamed before reaching for the phone while Midnight hurried upstairs. It didn't take her long to get ready, and she only slowed down long enough to text Tabitha before racing back downstairs to where Phil was waiting, his fur-lined hat tilted slightly back from his head and the chain mail beneath his tunic clanking as he moved.

Ten minutes later, they were at the garage, and Midnight caught sight of her mom's old Vespa sitting in one of the bays. Gone were the faded, peeling paint and rusted parts. Now it had a pastel yellow body, gleaming chrome, and off-white upholstery. She let out a soft gasp and Phil looked up in concern before realizing what had caught her attention.

"Looks a bit different, doesn't it?"

"I can't believe it's the same scooter," she said truthfully as she walked around it. Suddenly she understood just why Taylor had been so excited. "It's amazing."

"Thank you." Phil's round face lit up. He beckoned for her to follow him past the cars and spare tires to the back room. The place was filled with everything from an old-fashioned gas pump to gleaming swords. Along the back wall was a neat bench with long shelves filled with plastic boxes full of spare parts.

Phil carefully lifted the electro-pulse converter out of the bag and made a clicking noise with his teeth as he examined it. Then he grinned and reached for a screwdriver. Fifteen minutes later, he put down his multimeter and stepped back to admire his handiwork. It involved a small glass jar with a battery and some wire inside it.

"Okay, Midnight Reynolds. This is now fully

operational. When you press that button, a charge comes out through the brass pipe at the side. See?"

Midnight held her breath and watched Phil's oil-stained finger press down on one of the many switches. There was a humming noise as a red light lit up, and a small spark appeared at the end of the brass pipe. Phil's brown eyes filled with pleasure. Suddenly, Midnight could imagine Phil and George Irongate having a conversation about spectral transformers and the best way to solder a wire.

She also started to understand just why her mom and sister both liked him so much—and just how much she had misjudged him. After all, poor Elizabeth Irongate's stepmom had killed her. The worst thing Phil had ever done was tell the occasional lame Viking joke.

The two things could hardly compare.

"Phil, thank you. You have no idea what this means." She bowed her head to hide her burning cheeks.

"You're welcome. Oh, but just so you know, the battery will only last for five minutes of use. Whatever it is that you're using it for, you'll need to do it fast."

"Okay." Midnight nodded before giving him a shy

smile. "And thank you for not asking me what it's for."

"If I'm going to be part of your family, you should be able to ask me for help whenever you need it. No questions asked." Phil shrugged and wiped his hands with an old rag, then gave her a warm smile. "Unless, of course, it's with spreadsheets. I think I'll leave them to you."

"Well, I'm grateful," she said as she caught sight of the time and realized that if she wanted to stop Miss Appleby, she really needed to leave. She gave Phil another smile before she headed for the door.

"Hey, Midnight," he suddenly called out. "Don't forget your glasses. Your mom said that you can't see properly without them."

Midnight flushed as she hurried back to retrieve them. "She's right. There were lots of things that I couldn't see clearly before. Thankfully, everything's starting to come into focus now."

Then, without another word, she hurried out of his garage and down the street. As she went, she sent Tabitha a quick text to tell her that the electro-pulse converter was working and that it was time to go and kick some butt.

CHAPTER TWENTY-SIX

"Wow, go, Phil," Tabitha said fifteen minutes later as they both crouched behind Miss Appleby's shed. Midnight had filled her in on what had happened. "To think that for the last week, the answer's been sitting across the dinner table from you."

"I know. It was only because I was going to throw it out that he even saw it." Midnight shuddered and lifted George Irongate's invention out of her backpack before getting to her feet. There was a large moving truck out in front of the house and a trail of people carrying boxes out. Thankfully none of them had made their way into the backyard yet, and the large tank was still there, gleaming despite the dull weather.

Midnight took a deep breath. This was it—her chance to fix what she'd started.

"So, what's the plan?" Tabitha asked as they made their way across the dry grass.

"There's only enough charge in this thing to last for five minutes, so we have to be quick."

"Five minutes? Well, that's unfortunate." Miss Appleby suddenly appeared in front of them, waves of darkness swirling around her body like a black halo. Midnight's mouth went dry. Next to her, Tabitha's face turned pale. This definitely wasn't part of the plan. But she refused to give Miss Appleby the satisfaction of knowing how terrified she was.

As usual, Miss Appleby was holding her knitting in her hands. Her skin was more illuminated than ever as swirling waves of dark energy rolled off her shoulders. Midnight's skin crawled at the visual reminder of just how badly she'd messed up.

"Unfortunate for you, maybe," Tabitha growled, plastering on her mocking frown. "But not for us. We've got you."

"If you say so," Miss Appleby said in a serene voice, glancing at Midnight. "I'm impressed you fixed it. You really are a lot more resourceful than I gave you credit for. Unfortunately, it's all going to be a waste of time."

"What makes you say that?" Tabitha demanded.

"Because, as I'm sure you read in my dearly departed husband's diary, George's first attempt didn't work. Too bad I won't be around to witness your faces when you figure out that you wasted your precious five minutes for no reason."

"Don't listen to her, Midnight. She's just trying to spook you," Tabitha said, though it was obvious that some of her bravado had left her.

Midnight dropped to her knees and carefully put the wooden box down on the ground. This was her only chance to make things better. She pursed her lips and focused. She'd made so many mistakes, misjudged so many people. This time she wasn't going to mess it up.

She pressed the button and aimed the brass nozzle at the large tank. Next to her, Tabitha shifted from foot to foot and sucked in a sharp breath as the small red light blinked into action. A spark of light flickered out of the pipe in Midnight's hand. Miss Appleby didn't look concerned. Instead, she gave them both a polite wave before walking back toward the house for the final time.

"Go on," Tabitha urged. "Point it at the tank and free the spectral energy. Let them cross over to the Afterglow. It's now or never."

"It sure is," Midnight agreed as the light glinted off the tank. Suddenly she froze. The tank. She could see the tank. As in, there was no dark energy around it at all. The darkness had been around Miss Appleby, which meant there was only one place all the trapped spectral energy could possibly be. Her adrenaline spiked as she twisted around and aimed the nozzle in the direction of the large knitting bag in Miss Appleby's hand. It was covered in darkness. She pressed her finger down and watched the first spark of light hit it.

The old woman spun back around, her mouth open and her brown eyes bulging as she was engulfed in a piercing white light.

"What are you doing?" Tabitha's head swiveled, her eyes misted in confusion. "What about the tank? You only have five minutes to get this right."

"The tank's the mistake." Midnight shook her head, her jaw tight. "That's why it didn't work for George Irongate. Every ounce of spectral energy has been sucked out of it and into those balls of yarn she's been using."

"Stop it. Turn it off." Miss Appleby's face crumpled as the knitting bag fell to the ground. A seemingly never-ending amber blanket tumbled out and balls of yarn rolled in all directions, hissing and squealing as they went. Midnight's heart hammered in her chest as the white light engulfed them all. And suddenly the yarn and knitted blanket were gone. Thousands of beams of light exploded skyward in a riot of colors. "Please, you can't do this."

"I'm not doing anything." Midnight gritted her teeth as the white light continued to pump out. "You're the one who did it. You trapped all of those souls, stopped them from crossing over to the Afterglow—all so you could live longer."

Midnight's whole body shuddered as the machine jumped in her hands. Next to her, Tabitha craned her neck upward and gasped.

"I can see it. It's—"

"Beautiful," Midnight agreed as a pale pink shower of light skyrocketed into the air and out of sight. Finally, the white energy coming out of the nozzle fizzled away and Midnight's aching arms fell to her side. Miss Appleby was still as the skin around her cheekbones began to sink.

"No." Miss Appleby let out a final gasp as her hair turned to dust and her body tumbled in on itself like a set of dominoes. "Please…" she gasped, but the rest of the words were lost as her body crumbled to the ground in a pile of dust.

"Is that it? Is it really over? Is she *dead*?" Tabitha asked just as the brown, shriveled grass rippled back to life. Midnight let out a gasp. Arthritic, old tree trunks straightened their spines and their branches unfurled green leaves, while delicate creepers inched their way back up the once-bare walls of the house. The whole place rustled with noise as small birds chattered to each other. It was like the entire yard had woken up.

"I don't know." The words tore at her throat. Was Miss Appleby really gone? The excitement that she thought she'd feel deserted her. She'd released all of the trapped souls but she couldn't smile. It didn't feel like anyone had won. What if she'd killed Miss Appleby? What did that make her?

"What if you saved hundreds and thousands of spirits who've been trapped in a place where they don't belong?" a clipped English accent said. The pair of them turned around to see a well-dressed, middle-aged man walking out of the back door of Miss Appleby's house. His hair was neatly combed away from his face, and his shoes were so polished they were almost a mirror. "That's what you're thinking, isn't it?"

"How did you know that?" Midnight took off her glasses for one moment to check that the man was actually real. He was.

"Because like all protectors, I've been where you are now. I too have witnessed someone turn to dust when the spectral energy they've been misappropriating is released. But trust me, it will get easier."

"Protector?" Tabitha folded her arms and stepped closer to Midnight, her blue eyes filled with menace. "What's that? And by the way, who are you?"

"Forgive me. I'm Peter Gallagher."

"What?" Midnight's jaw went slack. "As in Peter

Gallagher from the ghost hunter app?"

"I actually work for the Agency for Spectral Protection. It's our job to ensure that spectral energy isn't misused." He handed them both a business card. "And you must be Midnight Reynolds."

"Um, yeah." She studied the card for a moment but apart from saying, Peter Gallagher, Esq., Director, it wasn't much help. "This is my friend Tabitha Wilson. But I don't understand how this is all connected to the ghost app."

"Ever heard of hiding in plain sight?" A small smile tugged at his mouth. "We created the app to draw out any potential protectors who could see spectral energy."

Tabitha nodded her head in approval. "That's completely genius."

"Thank you. And now I'd formally like to thank you for doing such a stellar job of neutralizing this woman. I also need to ask your forgiveness for being so tardy in discovering that there even was a Black Stream here in your delightful town. And yes, I can see that you both have lots of questions, so let me give you a quick rundown as my team dismantles the house. How does that sound?"

"Surreal," Midnight admitted as she looked over to the house. Several of the moving company guys were standing at the back door, their overalls replaced with black suits and round bowler hats. They'd been his team all along.

"As you may or may not know, when spectral energy is not allowed to pass across to the Afterglow, it attracts a more dangerous counter-energy called planodiume."

"Dark energy." Midnight nodded her head. "That's what George Irongate called it."

"Ah, yes. He was the inventor of this contraption I see." Peter Gallagher carefully lowered himself to the ground to examine the electro-pulse converter that was still sitting on the newly restored grass. "Reversing the polarity to release the trapped spectral energy. Very clever." He examined it with interest before seeming to realize that Midnight and Tabitha were still standing there. "But enough of that. Whenever planodiume's allowed to build up, the results are diabolical, as I'm sure you've discovered. So we at ASP spend all of our time ensuring that spectral energy can move freely across to the Afterglow."

"The snowflakes," Midnight said, thinking of all the small sparks of energy she'd been noticing everywhere. "That's what it's meant to look like, isn't it?"

He nodded. "That's right. It's quiet magnificent to see. It only becomes dangerous if it's trapped here on Earth longer than it needs to be."

"There are more people like Miss Appleby who use it to stay young?" Tabitha's blue eyes widened, though it was impossible to tell if it was with excitement or terror.

"Among other things. When spectral energy's trapped inside inanimate objects such as glass and metals, it can be used as a weapon. When people say that mirrors and certain items are haunted, they aren't too far from the truth. Then, there are those who collect planodiume and use it as a power source. It's our job to carefully monitor all the Black Streams around the world to ensure that spectral energy isn't getting unduly trapped."

"So why did it take you so long to find out about Berry?" Midnight wrinkled her nose and Peter Gallagher let out a reluctant sigh.

"Your Miss Appleby had been operating here since before we started keeping records, draining so much spectral energy that we didn't even realize it was a hot spot. However, as you responded to each one of our surveys, we could start collating a pattern to let us see how much energy had been drained from the Black Stream."

"I feel so terrible." Midnight bowed her head as her cheeks heated up. "The thing is that I never—"

"It's not your fault," Tabitha cut in, her lips twisting. "Midnight didn't know that what she was doing was dangerous, and as soon as she did, she was determined to fix it. Which, I might add, she totally did."

"It wasn't my intention to make you feel defensive," Peter Gallagher said. "The exact opposite. The fact that you successfully neutralized an operation that's been going on for so long is remarkable. It also leads me to my next question. As you might have realized, there aren't nearly enough people with our abilities to cover all the Black Streams, which is why I'd like you to consider joining us."

"Are you offering me a job?" Midnight stiffened. "Because the last time someone offered me a job, she ended up being a lying, cheating, one-hundred-and-fifty-year-old energy stealer."

Peter Gallagher seemed to be resisting the urge to smile. "Ah, yes. Your reluctance is understandable. But what if I give you full access to all of our archives? One hundred years of evidence has been collated, and you can then make your own decision."

"Archives?" Tabitha looked at him with interest. "You say you have detailed archives? Does that include all births and deaths as well as socioeconomic characteristics?"

"I think that goes without saying," Peter Gallagher said. He produced a small tablet from his suit coat and tapped at the screen several times before passing it over.

"Nice." Tabitha let out a long whistle before fixing him with her piercing gaze. "What are your thoughts about hiring people without the sight?"

"We're always interested in support staff," he assured her. He flicked to another screen and showed Tabitha another database. Before Midnight could look at it, she caught sight of a delicate slither of pink fog hovering around the upstairs window. Midnight froze, half expecting Peter Gallagher to see it, but he seemed as oblivious to it as Miss Appleby had been.

Her breath quickened as the pale mist gently drifted

toward her until it was so close she could almost reach out and touch it. Her heart hammered in her chest as the mist formed into a ball, and for one second, she could see the face of Elizabeth Irongate staring back at her.

Thank you. It is done, a soft voice echoed in her ear. Before Midnight could answer, the face disintegrated, and tendrils of mist spiraled toward the sky and out of sight.

"Wow, Midnight. This data's going to blow your mind. I mean it's unbelievable," her friend enthused before narrowing her eyes. "Hey, what's wrong with you? You look like you've seen a—"

"I'm fine," Midnight quickly cut in, shaking her head to clear her vision. "Just still trying to process everything."

"That's completely understandable," Peter Gallagher replied. The all-too-familiar sound of the ghost app sounded out from somewhere in his pristine suit. He gave them an apologetic smile as he studied the screen. "Sorry, a report in Japan that I need to take care of. I'll leave you both for now. Could you consider my offer and get back to me within a week?"

"Okay." Midnight nodded, and they both watched as he disappeared into the house.

"This has been a really strange day." Tabitha shook her head before grinning. "And no pressure or anything, but you are going to say yes to him, right?"

Midnight didn't respond, but as she looked up at the sky, to where the pale pink fog had disappeared, she was pretty sure there was only one answer she could give.

CHAPTER TWENTY-SEVEN

"Come on, Midnight. I know you like your glasses, but have you thought about getting some different frames?" Tabitha said on Wednesday as they sat in the far corner of the cafeteria, getting ignored by just about everyone. "I saw these awesome ones that have tiny skulls all around them. You're so lucky you have bad eyesight."

"You say the sweetest things," Midnight retorted as she finished her sandwich and grinned. "And thanks for all of your help on that other thing."

"That other thing that we decided we shouldn't talk about in school in case anyone overhears us?" Tabitha coughed.

"We're in the Siberia of the cafeteria. I don't think anyone's listening," Midnight said in a dry voice, though it was impossible not to smile. They'd met with Peter Gallagher three days ago to both officially join the ASP family, so flying under the radar was probably the best thing they could do.

"Good point. So how are you adapting to the new geography? Not quite as spacious as that long table in the middle you used to sit at with Sav and Lucy," Tabitha said as a red-haired seventh grader pushed past her chair. "By the way, where are they? I haven't seen either of them all morning."

"Are you guys saying that you don't know?" The red-haired girl sat down next to them, her eyes sparkling with news. "I thought that you were tight with those two."

"Not exactly," Midnight quickly said. "Why? What's happened?"

"Shoplifting. They stole some sweaters from the mall and got caught."

"What?" Midnight sat up straight. Spectral energy made sense. This did not. "There must be a mistake. They both get so much allowance each week, there's no reason for them to steal."

"People don't always steal because of money," Tabitha said. "My mom knew a woman at the tennis club who'd go to the mall and steal lipsticks and then drive home in her Mercedes. Sometimes it's for the thrill. Are you sure about this?"

"Um, yeah." The girl gave a decisive nod of her head. "I was in the office this morning, running an errand for Miss Henderson, when the police came in with a photo of them from a security camera. Isn't that the most amazing thing you've ever heard?"

"Yes, there's nothing I like better than hearing about other people's misfortunes." Tabitha pursed her lips. "And since you don't like when people talk about you, you should put a lid on it. Now scram."

"Grateful much?" the girl muttered, but all the same, she collected her books and scuttled away, leaving Midnight and Tabitha alone at the table.

Midnight was the first to recover. "I still can't believe this."

"I wish I could say the same, but those two have a sense of entitlement that follows them around a bit like Miss Appleby's black energy." Tabitha toyed with one of her many bracelets before studying Midnight's face. "Did you really not know anything about it?"

Midnight gave a resolute shake of her head. "Absolutely not. It just makes no—" She paused as she remembered the green sweater that she caught them looking at when they'd been at the food court. And the things that Sav said she'd paid for when she'd gone out of the changing rooms to get the white jacket for Midnight to try on. Or the earrings that Midnight didn't recognize. She let out a little gasp.

"I take it you've realized they did it," Tabitha said.

Midnight nodded. "To think that I only took the job with Miss Appleby because I was worried about how to pay for the ski trip, and the whole time they were stealing, I was trying to buy."

"If it's any consolation, I don't think there's going to be a ski trip this year. I don't know Lucy's parents at all, but I do know Sav's. There's no way they'll be happy about this," Tabitha said just as her phone beeped. She studied the screen and jumped to her feet. "That was Mrs. Crown. Would you believe that she's just found the death certificate for Arielle Jenkins?"

Midnight blinked. She had no idea who Arielle Jenkins was or why it mattered they'd found her death certificate, but she knew better than to argue. "Wow. You'd better go and see it." Thanks to Tabitha's persistence, they were the only pair to get an *A* on their local history project. Turned out it was the photos of the cemetery that had really made the difference.

"I'll be back in five minutes." Tabitha got to her feet and pushed her way through the crowd, a vision in black. Whenever Sav and Lucy had left her alone in the cafeteria, Midnight had always felt self-conscious, as if she'd accidentally stepped into a world where she didn't belong. But here, she was surrounded by people just like her. It was strangely relaxing. She adjusted her glasses and was just about to study one of the many books Peter Gallagher had given her when Logan appeared.

"Hey, Midnight. Do you mind if I sit down?" he said. Midnight's cheeks heated as she quickly put her elbows over the book to hide the title.

"Oh, um, n-no," she stammered before catching his disappointed look. "I mean no, I don't mind."

"Thanks. So, I was hoping to ask for some help with

that upcoming science quiz."

"Are you sure that I shouldn't be asking you for help?" Midnight said before realizing that she'd actually strung a whole sentence together.

"Let me guess, Tabitha snitched on me?" Logan twisted his mouth and it showed his dimples. Why hadn't she ever noticed them before?

"I wouldn't say snitched." A smile hovered on her lips. "But the word 'brainiac' might've been thrown around."

"Are you mad?"

"No, just surprised—but good surprised." Midnight gave him a shy smile. "Tabitha also mentioned that you were pretty nice."

"Really? That doesn't sound like her. Unless—" Logan let out a groan. "She told you about that black nail polish, didn't she?"

"It's possible." Midnight giggled. "But it makes you sound like a pretty cool study partner."

His eyes lit up. "Are you saying that you might want to hang out and study together sometime?"

"Yeah." Midnight gave a slow nod of her head just as the bell rang.

"Cool. I mean really cool. So, I guess I'll see you around."

"Okay." Midnight smiled and watched him leave. She started to gather her books up as Tabitha came hurtling back toward her.

"Did I just see you talking to Logan?" her friend demanded. "Were real words and full sentences used?"

"Actually, they were."

"Excellent." Tabitha nodded in approval, and they threaded their way out of the cafeteria. "And now when I'm at your house tonight for dinner, I thought we could discuss the new spreadsheet you're making to handle working for ASP."

"How do you know that I'm doing a spreadsheet?" Midnight started before coming to a halt. "And what's this about dinner?"

"Oh, your mom invited me to have a look at all the photos I took of the lemons she gave us. I told her they would look great on her blog and she agreed. I'm not saying that food photography is as good as going to the cemetery, but it's not bad," Tabitha explained before frowning. "And before you say it, it's not weird."

"It is a little bit weird," Midnight corrected, smiling. "But then again, I wouldn't have it any other way."

COMING FALL 2018:

MIDNIGHT REYNOLDS
AND THE AGENCY OF SPECTRAL PROTECTION

ACKNOWLEDGMENTS

As always, a big thank-you to my dear friends, Sara Hantz and Christina Phillips, for helping guide me through yet another book. You guys are the absolute best. I'd also like to thank Rachel Bailey for being wise and funny and always on hand no matter what.

Thank-you to Susan Hawk for being such a fan of this story and for being so patient as we worked to get it right!

I'd also like to give a shout-out to all my lovely colleagues at Napier Library who love books just as much as I do. A special mention to Mathew Clare who is the ultimate children's librarian and a nice guy to boot!

It's been such a joy working on this book and that's been down to Wendy McClure, Eliza Swift, Alexandra Messina-Schultheis, and the entire team at Albert Whitman. Thank you so much for providing Midnight with such a lovely home.

And finally, to my husband and kids, who've had the pleasure of being dragged into numerous brainstorming sessions, whether they've wanted to or not. See, I told you it would pay off.

CATHERINE HOLT was born in Australia but now lives in New Zealand, where she spends her time writing books and working in a library. She has a degree in English and journalism from the University of Queensland and is married with two children. She also writes books for older readers under the name Amanda Ashby and hopes that all this writing won't interfere with her Netflix schedule.